Flight of the Maita
Book five
Now You See It – Now You Don't

The crew are asked by Wahnee to investigate a planet that has disappeared – and they find one actually *has*!

Critic comment
I laughed my ass off. I REALLY like those golems, and they have to be used in more books.
– PA Rtng: Worth about ten times the price

Contents

About the author

CD was born in Lakeland, Florida, in 1938. He is educated in genetics and botany. He has traveled over much of the world, particularly when he was in music as a rock rhythm guitarist with some well-known bands in the late sixties and early seventies. He has worked as a high steel worker and as a longshoreman, clerk, orchidist, bar owner, salvage yard manager and landscaper – among other things.

CD began writing fiction in 1984 and has more than 300 books published as of 3/15/16 in SciFi, murder, orchid culture and various other fields.

He now resides in Puerto Armuelles David and Gualaca, Chiriqui, Panamá, where he continues research into epiphytic plants and plays music with friends. He loves the culture of the indigenous people and counts a majority of his closer friends among that group. Several have "adopted" him as their father. He funds those he can afford through the universities where they have all excelled. "The Indios are very intelligent people, they are simply too poor (in material things and money. Culturally, they are very wealthy) to pursue higher education."

CD loves Panamá and the people, despite horrendous experiences (Free e-book; *Fading Paradise*). He plans to spend the rest of his life in the paradise that is Panamá
- Estrelita Suarez V. de Jaramillo – 3/15/2016

CD is the discoverer of the Chadam Protocol for curing cancer.

Facebook page Ambrosia peruviana for cancer

Now You See It – Now You Don't

<u>*Disappearing Planet*</u>

The day was truly perfect, but then, they always were on Empire Center. It rained in the early hours of the morning – if you could call anytime morning on a planet with three suns, at least one of which was always in the sky.

Z (Steve Zutec, an Earthman) called it morning when the red sun set and the green one was still low in the eastern sky. Actually, he considered it morning when the green sun rose, afternoon when the yellow sun rose and night when the red sun rose.

The planet was one that had been placed by a race who were wiped out when they had a telekinetic backwash that burned their home planet flat when they moved the stars into their present positions. The stars were placed at the points of an equilateral triangle, with the planet now called Empire Center in the center of the triangle. The planet had been planoformed into a paradise before the stars were moved and colored.

The stars were moved by a mental gestalt that was amplified by a machine that had been placed on the planet. It was the most magnificent machine ever created by any race in the galaxy. It could move stars! Literally!

The race hadn't realized the use of such monumental amounts of energy couldn't simply be stopped. So far as anyone could figure – very few understood T.K. power at all – the use of mental gestalt on that order through the dimensional planal interfaces caused a flow of energy that must remain balanced between planes in a sort of pulsation. The "forward" pulse that had moved the stars (Nothing was actually moved. The stars were merely "shifted" in position on the point that is the N plane by passing them into and out of a neutral plane) produced a type of inertia on the interface that exhibited itself as energy coming from the interface, where there is no mass, at the point where the action was begun. (See? It made no sense to anyone but Thing, who found it rather simple and obvious.)

The action was movement of tremendous masses in the N plane – the reaction was the energy on the interface, which resulted in backwash.

They moved the stars to the exact orbits they wanted and suddenly ceased the gestalt. The energy flow backwashed and destroyed them.

The machine realized it had been instrumental in destroying its creators, and had gone insane. It put out a teleprojection that covered a sphere with a radius of eight plazsis (1 plazsi equals one Terran lightyear plus a bit more than a light week.) That projection was destroying several of the nearby (In the galactic sense) evolving cultures. Any organic life with a mind in that sixteen plazsi sphere was almost immediately a slave to those projections. It was doomed to stagnation, as a result. The situation was intolerable.

Z and his mixed bag of friends stopped the machine and brought two races to make permanent colonies on the planet and two others who just visited. Those people were felt by Z and his friends to have earned the right to some peace and plenty.

Another of the new sciences the planet had to offer was the transmat (Matter transmitter), which they used as a portal on each of several planets to move, without time lapse, from place to place. The machine caused an "alley" to open along the interface of two dimensional planes where one could step "past" a couple of dimensions from one point to another.

Z didn't understand it, and indeed, neither did anyone else. Except Thing, who thought it might understand some day.

They simply copied the original machine, with one major difference: The portals on Empire Center were controlled by the user through thought, while you had to have a "key" to go anywhere off the world. They couldn't figure out the intricate relays to make it work on the mental energy principal. The "key" was a computer that programmed your destination.

Maita, spaceship, computer and very close friend of Z and the rest of the crew, carried a portable portal aboard they could use anywhere – or anywhere they had tried it, so far. They didn't give the technology to the other planets in their empire (Yes, it was named the Empire of Maita, but that's another story) as the advanced technology used in it could well lead to other gestalt backwashes and other extinctions.

The people on EC, as they all called Empire Center, used the machines constantly, as did the ones who used them to visit, thinking nothing whatever of it, but the ones who knew it best seldom used it to go off-planet. They didn't fully trust it.

The two races on Empire Center were the Tendd and Joe's People.

The Tendd were a race of beings approximately four feet tall, furry, with large shiny eyes and long splayed fingers and toes. They were highly intelligent, natural communicators, and natural philosophers.

The other permanent race, Joe's People, were named after the being who established the colony. He had helped in the original overthrow of the Pweetoos that had eventually resulted in the establishment of the Maitan Empire.

Joe's People were also about four feet tall and were as furry, but were heavier than the Tendd, who were quite thin. Joe's People were just evolving. They weren't yet much more than semi-intelligent.

The Tendd had language, while Joe's People did not. As yet, they didn't even have greatly adapted vocal cords.

The visiting races were: the Parf, a strange race from a magnificently beautiful multi-ringed planet. The Parf were four-legged and two-armed, but were not centaur-like. They were feathered, the males brightly and the females more drably, and were highly artistic. They were very intelligent, had very complex languages, and even had developed spaceflight. The Maitan Empire showed them how to produce artificial gravity, as they were physically unable to tolerate much weightlessness. That opened the galaxy, or the small part of it that was now the empire, anyhow, to them. They were very highly respected by everyone they met.

The other race who had keys to visit were the Vendans, a seeded race of beings from the same stock as one original member of the group, called Ape.

Ape was seven four, but most of the Vendans were about six six to six eight. The best description Z could come up with was that of his first impression on seeing Ape. They looked almost like the Wooky in the old Earth movie, "Star Wars."

Ape was large and fierce in appearance, but was actually a very gentle being with an excellent sense of humor. Ape had taken a mate on Vendu. He now had his own family. He didn't travel with the group anymore.

Z had claimed an island on Empire Center and named it New Earth. He claimed it as his own, and was bringing many plants and animals from Earth to be re-established there. Earth was mostly flooded, due to the melting of the polar ice caps from hydrocarbon pollution of its ionosphere.

Z's father had grown orchids and bromeliads as a hobby, and his mother had raised parrots. He went to Earth, where he collected as great a variety of those plants and birds as he could find. Many were extinct on Earth, but his collection was as complete as any that had ever existed in any one place.

He hadn't brought whole plants back, but had taken small pieces of many varied natural species, which Maita then grew as meristem clones. They were then easy to transplant to Z's island.

The island was tropical, about three hundred fifty square kilometers in area, with an extinct volcanic mountain in the center. The mountain was quite high, so he could raise any of the plants somewhere along it. It was snow-capped most of the year, though there wasn't much change in the seasons and the snow was more thick frost.

He had become interested in camellias while gathering his orchids, so had planted several exceptional varieties higher on the mountain. They required almost exactly the same conditions as cypripedium and cymbidium orchids.

While in the area that had once been Florida on Earth he found some now low hills where Bok Tower once stood and there found a few coquinas and some sunray clams, which he quickly introduced along his shoreline. He was greatly surprised when they flourished.

Thing came up from the beach, riding the floater.

Thing was a small, squarish/globular, rubbery being with four tentacles in lieu of arms and legs. It had eyes on short stalks, which, disconcertingly, worked independently of one another. It was from a high-density planet, so enjoyed being in the deepest water, where it studied the life on the bottom. It was designing and planting its own underwater gardens. It was an empath who couldn't speak directly, so Maita had designed a circuit it could use to communicate with the others. Just before and just after each vocalization a clear middle "C" tuning fork sound ([–]) announced Thing's speech. Because Maita used the same speakers, there was a distinct difference in the tone it used. Maita's tone was a complex bell tone (* – *). As the tones came before and after their speeches, Z thought of them as quotation marks.

A problem – or one of a vast array of them – to those who hadn't been around the group much was that both Maita and Thing (And also Triss, a Tendd who Maita had "programmed" the Maitan language to) tended to speak without paragraphs, so their thoughts could change several times in one speech. Z was used to it now, so didn't notice. He listened to the words, not to the lack of inflection.

The floater was in constant contact with Maita, who, being a spaceship more than sixty meters across, couldn't very well accompany the people in its group whenever they were aground. It spoke through the speakers that Thing also used, as well as on all parts of itself and in most places on EC.

Thing was in fairly constant contact with Maita through its empathy, but Maita had soon opted to place separate computers on specialized circuits to handle Thing's vocalizations. Unless there was a special effort by one or both of them, the communication was cut off, except through the speech.

[Hello, Z,] Thing said. [I have been building a garden along the base of your island. It's too bad you will never be able to see it, as I know you appreciate beauty. I very much like the way you are planting the island. Is Tom here?]

Tom's with Tranz at the mountain, Maita said. *They

found a new series of caves they are spelunking.*

Tom was a being from the planet Zeena. It was far toward the center of the galaxy. Zeena wasn't a member of the empire, though some even farther in were.

Tom was a catlike being with coal black short fur and yellow slit-pupil led eyes. He had a tail, which the others sometimes kidded him about. Z often was amused by the name "Tom" on a catlike being.

Tom stood upright, as did the others (K-form, in Maitan classification). He was five four and extremely powerfully built. He could move so fast you couldn't follow him. He joined the group when they fought some pirates (Book 3, *Pirates*) and had stayed with them since.

Tranz was a Kheth. The Kheth had a federation of planets that was falling apart from the excess weight of its corrupt bureaucracy. They joined the empire to let the machines run the government for them in a last-ditch attempt to keep all their social and legal structure from totally collapsing and throwing them back into barbarism. It seemed to be working – so far.

The Maitan Empire was vast. It was run almost totally by machines, as they were more effective than any organic beings. They didn't get arrogant and self-important. Most cultures were unaware of that factor, because there was resistance among some races to being ruled by machines. A new system was steadily evolving to keep things running smoothly, and the few who knew that Emperor Maita was, in fact, a machine were keeping silent about it. In a generation, it would, hopefully, be forgotten.

The Kheth were of reptilian ancestry. They were very humanoid in appearance (K-form), but were hairless and had heavy-lidded slit-pupil led eyes. They had a fleshy crest across the top of the head and ears that were flat against the skull. The males were broad-shouldered with very small waists. They stood around six six. The females were much the same, but were an average of 6" shorter and thicker around the waist.

Tranz's parents, Sisstuh and Fesch, were diplomats for the old Kheth federation who had become fast friends with the group. They had asked the group that Tranz be allowed to travel with them for a trip or two. He fit in so well he decided to stay. He had joined the group only a short time before Tom and shared the experiences, since.

Tranz looked nearly identical to Sisstuh. He was an even tan/gray with a diamond-shaped patch across his chest in brown. It was a family trait.

"Why won't I be able to see it, Thing?" Z asked.

[Because it's three kilometers deep, there. Is Tous at the mountain? I would like his opinion about something.]

Tous is on the island, helping Z design an area around one of the waterfalls. Z wants to plant a lot of phalaenopsis orchids around it. I'm learning the names of your orchids, you see, Z. You could plant white phalaenopsis and maybe some pink aechmea-type bromeliads for contrast. Maybe fasciata. Larger rhipsalis and various ferns would add a great deal of texture to the overall view.

"Yeah, I'm planning to use both aechmeas and cryptanthus," Z agreed. "Trichopelia and Stanhopea orchids, a couple of the bigger Australian and Hawaiian tree ferns to the ocean side, with the fancy Vandas below them."

Tous was a Treen, or Parf. He had large dark eyes and a short rounded beak. The eyes were encircled with small flat feathers of a creamy white. He had a black and azure crest across the head and was eggshell blue over the rest of his body. He had vestigial wings that were almost unnoticeable, as the feathers blended so well.

He was a superb artist who once painted each of the

group. The paintings were hung in the private rooms in the mountain, now, but had been carried in the ship for some time. Maita's was, of course, still in the pilot's dome on the ship.

"Bess suggested some of the native fern types that'll grow in the cracks of the rocks," he said.

Is Bess here? I didn't know.

[Maita! You are supposed to monitor everyone who comes here! You are slipping!]

"Bess never went back to Parf," Z said. "He's been over working on a sculpture to give to the Tendd and Joe's People. He says it'll be in the middle of the lake and will have a platform around the base so they can use it as a swimming raft and deck. It'll symbolize the great friendship between the two very different races.

"Vech came by to criticize all of it as being ostentatious and overdone."

"That sounds like something Bess would say," Tous said as he came to them from the surrounding trees. "Vech lives to criticize."

[It's something Bess *did* say.]

Tous made his musical laugh. "Ah, yes! Our somewhat pretentious, but unquestionably great sculptor!

"Maita, I want a floater to go into the mountains to get some slabs of the pink marble, the black marble, the dark green marble and the very white marble. They are to be cut like this diagram and are to be thirty centimeters thick.

"Try to avoid any with cross grains, as there will be a certain amount of stress. I would hate it if it cracks. You can cut the back and sides with a laser, but I would prefer a very slightly roughened upper surface.

"I am a painter, not a sculptor, so am making a painting in marble to use as a wall for Z's domicile here. It will be truly superb in this setting! If I can place the colors as I see it, the suns will form contrasts and tonal mixtures that will take your breath away – even you machines who do not breathe!

"You can set the slabs in gold veining."

"Wait a minute!" Z cried. "Talk about pretentious! I'm not making a domicile here. I live in the mountain. You just ordered Maita to do a tremendous amount of work there!"

Tous shook his head, and insisted, "You said I was to design the large area on the side of the volcano around the mouth of the cave. I have designed it. The cave will be the domicile. The wall will face over the opening. I have already had Maita laser the walls flat and curved where I wanted, and have painted them properly.

"The outview perspectives and lines are excellently blended into the natural feature lines of this magnificent place. I have created a design I am sure you will like. Please let me finish. You can then be surprised and delighted with what I have done. It will blend to look as though it was formed when this beautiful place was created.

"Of course I'm pretentious! All we truly great talents are!" He giggled and went back into the forest path.

I have been working with Tous on this. I'm sure you will someday wish to bring a mate here to raise a family. Wait until you see what I have planned for you! I want to do this. Tous can finish the detail work when we are gone.

[Gone?]

"Uh-oh. What's up?"

The opposite of down. We have to make a call on a planet in the pirate sector. There are strange goings on.

[What kind of strange goings on?]

The planet seems to have disappeared.

"Disappeared?"

[Disappeared?]

Disappeared.

"When are we leaving? I've got to plant a couple of hundred orchids!"

[Orchids are tough. Tous will keep them healthy until we are back. You can depend on him.]

Z laughed, and answered, "I really hope so. One of our little excursions took eleven years!"

We will leave tomorrow. You can show Tous what to do, or, even better, you can have Triss's kids come here and let Tous teach them how to plant them for you. If you would have some of the young of Joe's People to come along, it would be to their advantage to learn some of the processes. Tous will oversee all of it so you know it will be right.

"I'll do that," Z answered. "I can use a little excitement about now – but only a little! That last deal was enough to last a long time, so far as excitement and adventure go!"

[I have enjoyed enough of that kind of excitement to last me a lifetime or two. Come along, Z! We don't want to keep the emperor waiting!]

"Maita doesn't have anything else to do anymore. It's got the empire running itself," Z pointed out.

They went to the portal, then on into the village of the Tendd, where Triss lived. Joe was there, so Z made all the arrangements for Atriss and Tirea, Triss's adolescent son and daughter, and two of Joe's People's adolescents to go to the island to learn. Joe's own children were too young to go.

Maita contacted Tous, who agreed to keep an eye on them. Tous would design the areas and would teach the youths to handle and care for the plants.

Z went to the mountain caves, where he waited until

Tom and Tranz appeared. Thing was already in the ship, so the rest of them went aboard.

*It has been more than a year since we did anything other than work on our dream world. We now have a problem and, as it *is* our empire, we must try to solve it. Personally, I can stand a bit of adventure and excitement. My machines do too good a job of running the empire. I feel useless. Do you know, I asked the main complex for information on weapons in our arsenals – and was told I didn't have clearance? Me? I'm the damned emperor!*

Tranz laughed. Z charged, "Your machines are becoming bureaucrats. That's just what the empire needs! Mechanical obstructive bureaucrats!"

Not any more! I shut that stupid damned thing down so fast I had it reprogrammed before its circuits were cold.

"What happens if one of your machines ever tries to take over?" Tom asked.

They aren't programmed to handle such a task. The secret of keeping control is to make a specific machine for a specific purpose. You don't use a machine for a purpose for which it wasn't intended. To do so simply asks for trouble.

"But suppose one of your powerhouse brain machines does try it?" Tranz asked. "We've twice had to deal with insane machines. I imagine they won't be the only ones."

I destroy the machine. Prepare for IDmode.

"How the nine hells do you prepare for IDmode?" Tom demanded.

Z said, "But they're like you! You can't just wipe out a machine without some kind of moral ... thing."

[Z, you raise cattle for a purpose. Is it morally wrong to kill them for food? Don't be silly.]

A better example is that you raise horses for friends and for use in personal pleasure riding. If a horse becomes dangerous, you shoot it. You can't allow it to bring harm to anyone. Is that also morally wrong?

"A horse is a different animal than a man," Z said.

A servo is a different machine than me.

"It's still a machine!" Z stated.

And a horse is still a mammal! Stop being obtuse merely because you are so good at it!

[You two stop it. We have some ridiculous anomaly that's a problem to our whole empire – and you two are arguing about servos and horses. That's stupid!]

"You're just jealous because your cattle argument didn't make any sense," Z replied smugly.

"Don't none of ya make no sense ta me," Tom drawled.

They often sparred to keep tension from building. Those who didn't know them would sometimes think they were going to come to blows. The reality was that it was their odd way of expressing deep affection for each other.

What I know is very little – don't even think of saying it! Wahnee, the ambassador for the federation at Fortney, has fastcommed an urgent message that a planet out near Tltle has simply disappeared. It was around a star called DX five, on our charts. The planet was surveyed from space and found to have a feudal-barbarian society. Mammals, you know. Swords and bows and spears. Many little holdings. Bronze age. Lots of wizards and magicians. Court intrigues. The normal thing for standard aggressive mammalian societies. It has a satellite monitor. Four of our days ago the monitor 'lost' the planet. It shows nothing there, anymore. Wahnee finds that puzzling.

[You *don't*?!]

Z said, "Near Tltle? That's one of our strongholds."

[I have a serious question. I don't know if you have all the information. Is the protector satellite still in orbit?]

Yes.

Tranz said, "Still in orbit? Then the planet's still there. You have to see it on some wavelength, even if there's cosmic dust or something."

"Maita said the satellite 'lost' the planet. It didn't say the planet was gone," Tom said. "Come on! A planet can't actually disappear without trace!"

*The planet's gone. A ship went right to the satellite and reported the planet is gone. It *did* disappear!*

"Oh, crap!" Z said. "If the planet was gone, the satellite would've moved off in a straight line. Ever hear of inertia? The planet's there, it's just invisible."

[Come on now, Z! How does one make a planet invisible? That's as bad as making it disappear and having a satellite orbit where it used to be!]

"I don't know how," Z replied. "I do know the planet's still there if the satellite's still there. Even with your two brains and all of Maita's circuits you can't show me how to orbit a satellite around space. As you so like to say, that's silly."

Tranz said, "I have a very chilling thought about how you can orbit a satellite around space.

"You collapse a planet into a black hole. The gravity's still there, but you can't see the black hole because it's only a couple of meters across, with that mass reaction."

An X-ray scan shows no black hole.

"I'm glad, because, if you can collapse a small object like a planet into a black hole...." Tranz suggested.

[I see what you mean. That would be a better weapon than even our antimatter.]

Z said, "Could it be a neutron mass instead of a black hole?"

A neutron mass is very highly reflective and would be about a kilometer and a half across with that mass. No.

Tom said, "Then I agree with Z. The planet's still there.

I can think of something that could have happened at that stage of development of a culture! I hope it's what I'm thinking! If it is, we're in for some great fun!

"It'll be dangerous, but it'll also be great fun.

"It could also be a strong T.K. power. We recently finished something with that basis."

There's no evidence of abnormal T.K. among the people. We are at Fortney.

They felt the twist.

The ship generally traveled in what was called sub-planal I(nter)-D(imensional)mode. It moved into another plane that contained all dimensions, but in a point. You didn't actually move in IDmode, you merely "jumped" across the point. The only time it took was resistance to time, itself. It was easier to "jump" many plazsis than to go a short distance. When they went into or out of IDmode, it disturbed the electrical flow in the mind, causing a twisting sensation.

They landed and went to the embassy offices, Thing riding on its special floater. It usually rode the floater — both for the speakers contained on it and because tentacles aren't very well-designed to move well on level surfaces. Tentacles weren't the best way to move without something to grip. It also rode around on one of the others quite often.

Z had once added, "Not to mention that you're immensely lazy!"

[Yes, but smart!]

"How smart is it to be lazy?" Z inquired innocently.

[I have a floater. You walk. Hup hroop hreep hore!]

They went into the offices, where Wahnee greeted them with hugs all around. Tranz said, when she finished, "How unlike a diplomat! Can't you conduct yourself in a manner more lending itself to proper...."

She laughed and pushed him down on the couch. "Kiss me, fool!" she cried.

Tom said, "You'd better watch it! He hasn't seen a Kheth woman in over a year."

"I finally lucked out!" she replied. "You people try to entertain yourself for the next couple of hours. Tranz and I have to discuss some things in private! Private things!

"Come on into my bedroom, big boy!"

They kidded around for a little while, then got down to the business at hand.

"The planet very simply wasn't there any more," Wahnee reported. "It's something that couldn't happen – but it did!"

"The planet's still there," Z insisted.

"We've looked. It's not there," Wahnee shot back. "I went to see for myself. The sun's there, but the world is *not*!"

Tom asked, "Was the satellite there?"

"Surely!" she said. "We homed on the satellite."

"Then, don't you see?" Tom cried. "The planet's there, or the satellite wouldn't have anything to orbit around!"

"We'd thought of that. We cannot detect any planet," she countered. "We tried every different type of sensor we have. There's nothing there! That planet had several million people on it. People who will someday develop into one of the better races.

"There is the gravity of a planet, but no planet. This is one problem that *has* to be solved!"

[Did you go to where the planet was? I mean, physically go there?]

Wahnee laughed. "We flew directly through the core of any planet that might have been there. It is *not* there! I know you don't want to believe it, but it's a *fact!*"

That was the first thing I was going to do. Go to the exact center of that planet.

Tom was laughing. Z joined him.

[What's the matter with you two fools?]

Z said, "I think I know what Tom expects to find. There are two ways it could be done."

Tranz said, "Two ways what could be done?"

"One way would be real, Tom," Z said. "Which do you hope it is?"

"I want it to be real," Tom replied. "Oh, how I want it to be real!"

Z turned to Wahnee. "Did you take the satellite apart?" he asked.

"Why?" she asked. "What's the point?"

"You'll see!" Tom said. "We have to go take that satellite apart, Maita. That will settle one question.

"Oh! I hope the satellite's in perfect condition. I really want nothing more than for that satellite to be working just as perfectly as ever!"

Are you serious?

Z said, "Very serious. For two excellent reasons. One's because, if the satellite's working right, the people are all perfectly safe."

[And the other?]

"You'll see!" Tom rejoined.

They talked awhile, then went back to the ship, then to the place the planet was supposed to be. Soon, they were alongside the satellite, having come to its beacon. They couldn't see any evidence of a planet, though it should cover more than half the sky in one direction at that distance. There was a clear, starry background.

"How did you find the satellite?" Tom asked.

It broadcasts a signal. All I have to do is home in on it. That's how Wahnee got here.

"I wonder where we'd be if you'd gone by MGS coordinates instead of homing on the satellite?" Tom said.

[Where do you think we are?]

"Maybe on the far side of the sun?" Z answered and laughed. "I hope not!"

I get the feeling we have been put on. The satellite is at the exact MGS coordinates where we are supposed to find it.

Tom exclaimed, "Oh, I sincerely hope it's not one single millimeter from where it's supposed to be!" and he and Z started laughing.

[I get the strange feeling that I also hope we are being tricked, this time.]

Maita sent a floater out to bring the satellite into the hold and the group went in to inspect it. Z took the panel off the side and they checked the circuits.

"What are we looking for?" Tranz asked.

"A little whatzit to make the satellite take an eccentric orbit around the star," Z replied.

Maita had a servo-mech attached to the satellite to check everything inside the case. *It's in perfect working order. There's nothing whatever wrong with this satellite. We are the first to open it since it was placed. The seals were unbroken. It's Zeenan, so there is nothing whatever wrong with the thing!*

"Oh, good!" Tom cried.

They put the satellite back in orbit.

[I now agree with Tom and Z. The planet is still there. What's the big joke, guys?]

Z said, "We've got to go to the planet. We can't do it.

"This is the joke – we've got to work out a way to get to a planet that isn't there when we're there, or something that's equally neat!"

What do you mean? The planet is either there or it isn't there.

Tom answered, "It's there. Just not when we are. I think maybe that's how it was done. Would you agree, Z?"

[That's what Z said!]

Z said, "Yeah, Tom. Time displacement?"

"As likely as anything," Tom replied.

Tranz said, "You two clowns stop it! What the hell is going on?"

Tom giggled and said, "We called him Frezzwin."

Z said, "We called him Merlin."

[I'm calling a stop! What are you two halfassed idiots talking about here?]

Tom said, "I'm going to tell you a story, then Z will tell you a story. No doubt Triss could tell you one, too. Probably almost any race has the stories. I doubt that Joe could, yet. He's about six thousand years from it.

"Once upon a time, there was a strong – though quite small – kingdom. It was rich and kindly to those around it, but it also could be brutal to those who opposed it. That's often the way of civilizations at that stage of development.

"The king was young. He was a predicted king.

"The wizard, who had served two kings before, said, at his birth, he was destined to fame for all time. The proof of his worthiness would be that he would be the only person on the face of Zeena who could draw the magic Bow of Chants. This bow would make him the fiercest and best warrior of all time.

"When the boy, named Thuus, was just reaching the age of adulthood, he was in the dark Forest of the Dead by the base of the Mountains of Doom when he chanced upon a beautiful jeweled bow. It was in the open, with the string around a mushroom-shaped rock.

"The boy, Prince Thuus, saw that the string wouldn't pass over the top of the rock, so he decided to cut it. He wanted that Bow!

"He had the best of knives, but the string would not cut. The only way to get the bow off the rock was to draw it and lift it over in the bowed configuration.

"He called his head bow master over and instructed him to remove the bow for him, but the huge giant of a man couldn't draw the bow.

"The prince became exasperated and asked the wizard to cast a spell to remove the bow. The wizard said this was the famous Bow of Chants. It was proof against spells, which so angered the young prince that he strode to the bow, drew it, and lifted it from the rock, fulfilling the ancient prophesy. The prince became the most famous and fairest king of all time. He was served faithfully by the wizard, who did many things.

"The wizard could stop the sun in the sky.

"The wizard could hide the world from the night dragon.

"The wizard could make the world and all things in it disappear.

"This story is a myth of our people, but we've found some evidence the kingdom really did exist.

"The wizard was called Frezzwin. No other wizard will ever equal him in power.

"Z?"

Z said, "The story on Earth was much the same. The wizard was called Merlin. It was the Singing Sword. It was at King Arthur's court.

"The Singing Sword was fixed into a solid rock, and only the chosen could pull it out. Same story. Some archaeologists have found evidence of Camelot, the palace of King Arthur. It wasn't the magnificent structure of the tales, but none were at the time the story supposedly took place.

"There are legends of another great magician on Earth. He was known as Apollonius of Tyana. He's even found in the court records of the time. I suppose all mammalian races have such a magician at some time in their history.

Perhaps it's an unconscious race gestalt that's a part of the developing mind, or perhaps it's some kind of being who goes to the better races and lives among them for a period of time at a certain point in their evolution.

"When we find a way to that planet we're going to find magic is in full swing! Magic that's really magic – and that works! It's probably some wild T.K. talent, but magic always has humor as well as great danger with it. It has the awe and the audience. A good magician is a good show-man. That's why Tom and I expect some fun.

"Merlin was powerful, and could be deadly, but he wasn't evil. I'd think the same is true of Frezzwin.

"Apollonius stood up against tyrants. They couldn't harm him. It's documented in the records he stood up to the mad emperor, Nero, and didn't suffer for it. He didn't die, but simply vanished from a courtroom after lecturing the high councils and the emperors that they were all corrupt fools. In front of many people, he vanished. He appeared on an island over a hundred miles away on the same date. It's in the records.

"This was only a few years before the time of Christ. The fastest form of travel on land was horses and in water was sailing vessels. There was no way he could've gone a hundred miles across both land and water in less than five days."

[Then you are saying the same being – or at least the same force – is at work here? This disappearing planet is simply a magician's trick, a standard sort of thing in your legends?]

"I would say so," Tom agreed. "The planet's hidden from the dragon of the night or something on that order."

And how is that done?

Z said, "By displacing the planet in time. That would be my guess! We know damned little about time, as you constantly remind us."

Oh, really! That isn't possible! How much time?

Tom laughed and said, "The transmat isn't possible. You can't use the interface between dimensions. It's against every theory ever proposed. Still, we use the transmats. We move between dimensional interfaces."

Z replied, "I'd say the time displacement is a hundred billionth of a second or less. Any displacement at all means it's not there when we are."

[I say they are right about much of it, Maita. It's magic and that sort of stuff, but the planet isn't displaced in time. I refuse to believe that for one billionth of a second or less! A much simpler way is used to hide it. I want you to calculate the exact center of the planet from the satellite's orbit. Tell me when you have it.]

They waited about ten minutes and Maita said, *All right. I have the center.*

[Fire two missiles you can track, both visually and through other methods. Fire them at exactly the same moment from a few degrees apart from satellites. Have them aimed and timed to run together at the planet's center. Don't make them explosive or anything like that. If they hit the planet, we don't want a lot of damage. It's merely a test, not an attack.]

Maita flew three missiles out instead of two. and aimed them all for the center of the planet to impact together there.

The missiles were fired. They were tracked and watched. The missiles went to the point that should be the center of the planet and hit together.

Now what?

[I timed them. Did you?]

There was a pause. *Forty seconds too much.*

[Shall we now go to the far side of the planet to check

the debris?]

*Whoa! A null inertia field? That *big*?! Great exploding galaxies! I think I much prefer even that ridiculous time displacement theory! Do you have any idea of the power it takes...?*

[Yes. Null inertia. Induced. It doesn't break any laws of physics, as we understand them, it merely demands a science we don't have.]

Tranz asked, "What does that mean?"

Everything, including light, is being diverted around the planet. The inertial force is canceled, so no instruments will record the bending of the trajectory.

[The planet's still where it was. The light that's inside the field will stay for a good while, but it will slowly get darker as the light's absorbed. They will pop back into our view after a time.]

Z said, "We'll have to find a way to land. It may be days before they pop out."

Maita said, *I will make a null field and we can go right in.*

[How will you do that?]

I don't know. Yet.

Would all of you please come to room two?

The group had been in their private spots, resting, while Maita tried to solve the problem of landing on the planet.

Maita was what would be called a "flying saucer" type of ship back on Earth, where Z was abducted. It was circular and flattened with clear domes on the top and bottom. There were ten rooms with five cubicles behind the outer walls of some of the rooms.

The clear dome on "top" of the ship was called the O dome, while the dome below was the pilot's dome. The domes could, of course, be opaqued, should conditions dictate.

The pilot's dome was reached by an elevator with its own gravity grid in the floor, as the dome was "upside down" to the rest of the ship, meaning the elevator had to revolve or you would stop with your head at the floor. It was a unique experience they exposed all newcomers to, just to watch their reactions.

People outside could watch them moving around on the "ceiling," if the dome was clear. It made for good effects, in certain circumstances.

Z used the pilot's dome for his private quarters. It had an infinitely adjustable seat in which he could be totally comfortable, as well as complete sanitary facilities and dining facilities. The various head gears could also be used to learn, calculate, design, or almost anything else. Everything happening in or near the ship could be monitored from the pilot's chair. There were several holovid screens, meaning more than one project could be working at the time.

Room one was the entrance port and cargo hold. It was

the largest section of the ship. It contained a complete shop and laboratories, as well as storage and stasis chambers. They had long ago installed eighteen of the power spheres (most ships had only one) in the hold. Each sphere contained the energy of a medium-sized hydrogen bomb.

Room two, where Maita had just called them, was called the medical and instruction room. There were all sizes of padded benches and consoles for the teaching or "reading" of organic and inorganic beings, alike. The group had taken those benches most comfortable to the individual and made a circle around the main console, which had a large holoscreen above it. They held most of their conferences there, though they could communicate throughout the ship with no problem. They had found it better to be together when working on problems, because they got more ideas.

The medical boxes could "build" a body from raw elements, though making a working brain was another question, altogether.

Z, Tranz or Tom could be quickly modified greatly in appearance in the medboxes, but Thing couldn't, because of extreme internal pressures and critical organ size and shape. Maita very cautiously made any modifications, as it was also in the learning stages of that science where a mistake could prove fatal.

There was a cubicle behind room two they called "Doe's room," after an Immin female who had once used it. It had a comfortable bench and a headgear that was directly attached to the ship's "library," as well as containing all the usual facilities of an efficiency apartment. Thing used that cubicle as its own private quarters when it wasn't with Z in the pilot's dome.

Tranz and Tom both stayed in room nine when they were

on the ship. It was a bunk room from the original users of the ship, had all the facilities they could want and more, and was plenty comfortable.

Food and drink was manufactured and delivered to any of them at anytime anywhere on the ship. Maita could "build" the food an atom at the time for them, thus eliminating toxins and such nasty little surprises from their diet.

They sat on their favorite benches. Thing climbed into Tranz's lap.

I have found it most interesting to work on a problem like the inertia field. I think I have found a way through it. We will land where we find an appropriate spot. The old federation had language crystals, which you will find on the console tray. There are six or eight major languages, but they are from only two roots, so you can wear just the two crystals and will have complete cross-referenced use of the languages. You will see the customs aren't unlike those of many feudal societies we have seen. The people seem to be, as Wahnee said, capable of evolving into one of the better races. We must be most careful to avoid cultural interference and damage here. We will simply ascertain that things are all right, then go. Insert the crystals. You will see much about them.

Z and Tom had small sockets in their earlobes that were wired directly into their brains' communications centers. Any language could be implanted in a crystal that looked much like a perfect diamond. Placing a crystal into the socket gave them the full use of the language – written and spoken – as well as the customs. Other crystals could contain an endless array of information and skills.

The crystal's removal from the socket left them with no retention whatever of the information on it, but Maita's other machines could extract certain things and program them directly and permanently.

Tranz had the sockets in small invisible slits in his neck, as he had no ear lobes. They each had one other socket behind the ear (and on Tranz's neck and a tentacle base on Thing) that activated a grid etched into their skulls if the crystal was removed from it. That grid stopped dangerous mental influences, such as teleprojections, against them. They had elected to be able to turn off the grids, because Thing, being an empath, couldn't long survive without mental contact.

Any crystal in the socket turned the grid off.

I don't know if your magician, should he exist, is a mentalist. Be ready to remove the crystals should it prove necessary. We are going in. Would you rather go to a dome or would you prefer that I project onto the big holo-vid?

Z said, "Project. You can zoom in on any area we like, that way."

The others agreed.

Oh, good! It works! We are in the atmosphere. I'm just staying high enough to where I can't be seen except possibly as a reflection point.

[You mean to say you didn't even know if it would work, and you called us here?!]

You had to waddle for less than five meters! What's the big deal?

"Yeah," Z said. "What do you want? A floater to ride around on in the ship?"

[That would be nice. Maita?]

Forget it!

"Tranz and I had to come all the way from nine!" Tom said, "and Z came all the way from the pilot's dome. *We* don't need a floater!"

[Hrup, hroop, hreep, hore!]

Tranz said, "I would really like to see you riding on a floater in that elevator. The elevator could turn and you could float out of it upside down and fall on your ass."

[In the first place, the floater has its own gravity. In the second place, I don't have an ass. You will never get that right!]

Sometimes you are an ass all over. Are we going to snip at each other or look the planet over?

"I vote to snip at each other," Tom said quickly.

"Me, too," Z replied.

[I vote to snip.]

"I'll go along with the majority," Tranz said.

Awright! Knock it off!

[Knock what off? Of what?]

"Knock you off. Of that floater," Tranz replied, tossing Thing to Z. "We'll be good, Mom," he finished.

Thing wrapped its tentacles around Z, pinning his arms to his sides. [Help! I'm being attacked!]

Tom said, "Who's attacking you? I'll help them!"

Stop it! We aren't here to have fun!

Z laughed as Thing released him and went to his lap. "Ha! We're going to have a lot of fun here, Maita. Loosen up," he said. "That's what Tom and I were talking about all the time. It's fantasy time! All your wildest fantasies can now become real! Come to Tlorg! Live in the age of magic!"

[You are weird! Well, even more than usual. A little. Maybe. Very strange, at least.]

The view was amplified and cast on the wall behind the console. It showed mostly rolling hills and patches of forest, with mountains in the background.

Let's find a place to land down there, then we can see if we are going to have any fun.

"Can you find where the inertia field's coming from?" Z

asked.

No. It's nondirectional and is only a few meters thick, perhaps a hundred meters above the atmosphere.

"Let's find the richest castle on the planet, then," Tom said. "It'll have the strongest wizard."

There isn't any castle on any other continent. This is a fairly large one, though, and will take some time to search.

"Why search?" Z asked. "Just go high enough so you can see a large area. Scan it for towns or larger castles with towns inside the walls, then go to another area. Back the view toward the ship until it shows only larger details. Find us one we can land at without being too far away, but one that's fairly large and prosperous."

The view expanded while the details shrunk as though they were flying away from the planet.

"Stop," Z said. "How many square kilometers do we see at this range?"

Around two thousand.

"There's only one castle and two little towns in that area," Z said. "Even that'll be slow.

"Can you scan larger areas with your equipment and pick out the details? You can zoom in on special features."

I can cover the continent with twelve scans, taking six minutes per scan. Come back here in an hour.

They left room two and returned an hour later. There was a projection on the wall. It was an island. They could see from the apparent size of objects that it was large. It seemed to be the sort of place that would attract population centers.

[Are those areas by the mountains towns?]

Yes. I feel this island is the best bet, here. I get very strange sensor readings. It also contains several large castles and some fairly large towns. The island is almost a hundred ten kilometers long by thirty four wide. It also contains some very rough mountains and two major rivers. The climate is mostly mid-temperate. I get the strange readings from that large town there and somewhat less of them from the town about sixty two kilometers east of it. There are spots with anomalous sensor inputs all over the world.

"What kind of strange readings?" Z asked.

Dimensional planal nexi overlap in small spots. They don't last long.

Tom giggled and looked knowingly at Z.

Don't start! Tell me what's happening down there.

"The sorcerers are calling demons," Tom said.

"I think you may be right, Tom," Z said. "Our own transmats prove the mind can reach other planes. I wonder if they really *can* call demons?

"I'd like to meet one – I think. Maybe not!"

Tranz asked, "What are the people like? Can any of us go there and mingle? In some disguise?"

Tom said, "We'll go as we are, except the floater will have to be made to look like it.... Hey! Thing can be the head and the floater the body! The head can move around independently! It return to the body whenever it wants! That would be wild!"

[I don't know what they are talking about. Show us what the people here look like, Maita. Try to get some sense into this, somehow!]

"They look something like the Cheeth!" Z cried.

[Yes they do.]

The beings were quite humanoid, hair on the head, but with bushy eyebrows that made a straight line across the forehead above the eyes. The noses weren't as sharp or hooked as the Cheeth (A race Z and Thing had met) and they weren't quite as thin.

[The Cheeth would be a lot like that, Z. I'll bet they have the same legend.]

"Almost surely, if they're mammals," Tom said.

[They are. I don't think the legends are restricted to mammals. I've heard much the same thing from others.]

Where do we land?

"On the mountains overlooking that large town and castle there. Its base is only a couple of kilometers from the town," Z said. "There's that other one by the ocean. We can go there later if this one isn't what we're looking for.

"The trouble is, we'd have a hard time finding a place to land where you wouldn't be noticed. I've got an idea about that! Let's wait 'til tonight when it's dark and.... Oh."

[Yes. It won't get dark unless they drop the field.]

Tom said, "Land on that peak that overhangs a little. It looks stable enough. Come in through that cut away from the town where you won't be visible from down there at all. I sorta doubt there's anyone up there while the sorcerer has the world hidden."

Maita sat on the promontory. It was about a kilometer in altitude on a small mesa-like area. The sheer cliff dropped off almost to the base of the mountain. It was all granite, so was strong and solid.

"Now put up a dense smoke screen around us and set a crane to build a castle out of fiberglass like we used on Frim. Make it spectacular and an intense white. Lots of towers," Tom said. "Maybe you can condense some moisture to make it look like a cloud sitting here. That should be common enough to this kind of place."

That will take some time. How big a castle do you think we'll need?

Z said, "Just make an outer shell for now. You can make an interior anytime. It should be a bit larger and finer than the castle down there on general principles. We want to make their sorcerer curious and maybe a little afraid of us."

The winds here will blow it away.

[Are the bins still filled? Cast a hard metal framework anchored into the rocks. You can put lead or something in the fiberglass to give weight.]

"There're probably lots of minerals in these mountains. Use gold. Make it gold, instead of white," Z said. "That'll get the wizard's attention!"

We aren't in view from down there, here. I'll wait with the smoke until I have the materials gathered. There's a great deal of gold not too far. It's in quartz, so I can make the fibers from that.

"Is there a lot of onyx or black marble around?" Tom asked.

Yes.

"Inlay the floors with patterns of rose quartz – you'll have plenty of that from the gold mine – and black marble. That ought to impress everybody!"

[And Z said Tous asked too much of Maita!]

It's all the same to me. I send out squads of servos to do the work.

"So there!" Z said.

[Where?]

Are you going to start again?

They joked around for a few hours while Maita gathered large piles of pure gold and silica, which it placed in a slide from higher up the mountain and back from the edge. The crane was unfolded and placed so the building materials would keep the feeder-hopper filled by gravity.

Maita had a grid it called an elementizer, which broke the atomic bonds between unlike atoms, leaving pure elements. You dumped anything at all in the top and elements in pure state came out the bottom. The resulting elements fed directly down into the crane's intake.

The crane began spinning the castle with its coating of pure gold while Z, Thing, Tranz, Tom and Maita got into a very complicated game of Demons and Dragons, a game much like Stars and Comets. The game could last as much as ten days. It was complicated. Thing almost always won.

About two ship's days later, it started to get dark.

Z was with Tom on the edge of the cliff, looking down at the town through a pair of very good binoculars.

"The sun's setting," Tom noted. "They've dropped their inertia field."

The people in the pretty town went to bed that night with everything back to normal since the dropping of the field. In the morning, they woke up with a huge bright gold palace with six towers looking down at them from the cliff.

It was only the facade that faced the town, of course. Even Maita had limits, but the cranes would have the complete shell finished in two days and nights.

They waited and viewed the town far below. Several people set out to climb the cliff, but none came close. The afternoon of the third day Maita called them all to room two.

Okay. I've gone along with all this and have used almost a whole sphere's power to build this castle around me. It's probably ostentatious and gaudy enough for the most vulgar of tastes.

They'd left a large interior patio that Maita was in – or under, really.

You two seem to have some kind of plan. You say we can go into town as we are. What's the next step? Assure me we won't do any cultural damage to these people.

"You won't do any damage. We won't," Z said. "We'll be

some more demons. They're used to seeing them. They won't even think much about us, probably."

"Finish the castle as we planned, then we'll go into town to call on the local wizard," Tom said. "Don't be surprised at anything you see or hear. We want to know all we can about this, so let Thing's floater carry a number of sensors you can secrete around. You might want to set up a servo to monitor them, as we'll want a lot of them. We want to know everything that goes on in that castle as well as in some of the public houses here. Audio and video. We'll try to get inside the wizard's private laboratory, but probably can't. There will be things to keep us out."

What kind of things?

Z said, "Spells, demons, that sort of thing."

I doubt they will affect me much. I can even shield T.K. You should all remember your special sockets. If there's T.K. here, it could get dangerous.

"Then you're placing yourself in a dangerous spot," Tom warned. "We said this will be great fun – *and* that it'll also be dangerous. Don't underestimate what can be done with these methods. It isn't really T.K. I'm not at all sure you can shield it."

I'm not open to those suggestibilities.

Z said, "You're about to learn it isn't all suggestion. Believe me, Maita, I don't want to see you damaged or any of us hurt. Because it'll be fun is no reason to take it too lightly. It'll be fun for Tom and me, because we've always had a secret desire to swash some buckles."

Tom giggled and Thing demanded, [What in hell are you talking about?]

Tom said, "This is a secret dream of our species. We want to go back to relive the bygone days of knights and honor and horses and dragons and princesses and magic. We know it was actually a bloody, dirty, violent time, but it's also become idealized in our minds.

"We can be a part of this! We can be sly and devious and knightly – and all of it!

"Tranz will be the wizard, I think, Z."

"Yeah," Z replied. "He's the right height. The tallest one should be the wizard. He can wear black – no! White! – robes with a lot of symbols worked into them in pure gold thread. He'll be carrying a Pweetoo stun wand – all the wizards on Earth had their magic wands – with his personal power symbol worked into the end. The robes will be voluminous. He'll be wearing magic rings on most fingers. They'll be the finest, purest diamonds and rubies. One large emerald and a black opal the size of a golf ball (*A what?*) carved into his power symbol on a fine rhodium gold chain around his neck. Put several very small antigravity discs under the robes so they can do strange things.

"He could be wearing an antigravity belt! He can rise above the situation. Literally!

"Thing will ride a floater with a robe hanging from it to brush along the ground. The robe will sit under him as though he's the head of some monster. The robe can be tied around the 'neck'. The 'head' can leave the body at will. If we need a diversion, we can have one of us push the robe aside and walk under Thing. The body has no substance!

"Tom and I will be demon bodyguards."

Tranz said, "I won't know how to handle things. I won't know what to say!"

"Okay." Tom replied. "You'll be much to important to speak where.... No! You don't talk, because there's a spell that can steal your voice and use it against you if a certain demon ever hears you speak.

"I'm your demon bodyguard. Z's your demon voice. He

does all the speaking for you. We'll only communicate with one another in Maitan, and only Z will speak the language here. The demon can't steal Tranz's voice if it doesn't understand the magic language.

"What did you say these people call this world, Maita?"

Tlorg.

Z said, enthusiastically, "Let's design our costumes and go into town tonight. Maita can set up a large floater to carry us.

"How about some ... there's a word for a giant clam in the language, Maita. How giant is the clam?"

Maybe two and a half meters across.

Z laughed and said, "They're going to have a giant clam six meters across and two meters thick come and sit down in the area by the fountain in front of the castle! The clam's going to slowly open to reveal our select little group sitting on soft velvet and satin cushions. We'll step out of the clam and it'll again close. It'll resist any of their efforts to open it.

"If the wizard decides to open it, I'm sure he can, Maita. Resist him honestly and see."

[I suggest we design our costumes, eat, clean up and rest until night's ready to fall. Might I suggest we have some soft indirect lights inside the clam? Lights that seem to have no source?]

Tom said, "Good thinking, Thing! You're getting right into this."

They spent the rest of the day preparing for the night's plan. Z had a lot of gold chains and jewelry and a belt with a large jeweled wide-bladed knife stuck into it. Tom had the ever-present sheath knife of the Zeenan strapped to his calf, where he almost always carried it, and a thin sharp sword in a scabbard on one side with a widebladed knife with a double edge in the belt at the other side. They prepared a "tug" type floater from Maita's hold with a fiberglass shell that was pure white and just translucent enough to seem to glow.

On an idea from Tranz, they put a low table in the center of the clam and placed some silver and gold jeweled goblets, along with a crystal decanter of clear burgundy wine and a tray of exotic fruits. The seats were modified into four divans that radiated out to the edge of the clam. The group would be seen reclining and enjoying fruit and wine when the clam opened.

The power symbol was a triangle of silver, with leaves of gold angling off the sides. The tip of the triangle was the stun wand tip, while the shaft was designed to look like an arrow with the tip at the triangle point. The symbol was put in the top of the clam in pure gold, both inside and out.

They abandoned the idea of carving the opal to that shape, as it would be too much of a waste. Instead, the opal was made perfectly round and the chain which carried it was made of links in the form of the symbol. Tranz's robe had a hood that covered the head with a black cloth across the front. The cloth was so woven that Tranz could see out unobstructed, but none could see in.

Z changed that. "It's too easy. The least magician knows that trick and uses it in the blindfold bit. It would make us seem to be cheap tricksters, not demons and magicians.

"We had sunglasses back on Earth that were mirrors on the outside, but you could see clearly from inside. It might be interesting if they looked into Tranz's face and saw their own looking back at them!"

I can do way better than that! It will be on the same principal, but the mirror will be a screen and a camera hidden in the turban will actually project their faces onto it in full color. That should get their attention!

They designed that and tried it out. It worked perfectly to

where Z was a little startled at the quality. The screen was curved, so the projection was fully three dimensional and natural-looking.

They then went to their private spots, cleaned up, ate and rested until Maita called them to suggest it was fast approaching the moment of sunset in the village. Time to go!

They climbed into the clam. Maita floated them serenely down into the courtyard by the fountain. The top of the clam opened slowly and they finished their drinks, then stood to let themselves out of the shell. It quietly closed as they strolled toward the fountain.

What's going on here?

"What do you mean?" Tom whispered back.

They aren't at the least shocked to see us here! This is amazing!

"A sorcerer and his familiars? Of course not!" Z replied, with a grin. "We told you! They see demons all the time.

"You do know what this means, though, don't you?"

What, oh great evil one?!

"They really *do* call beings from the other planes!" Tom replied. "Think about it!

"We aren't evil sorcerers. We're here to rid them of evil."

People would get out of their way, but didn't seem unduly surprised by them. They were fairly much avoided.

[What do we do?]

"Walk around the town and look everything over," Tom answered. "See the layout of the town. Try to locate where the wizard stays if he's not in that ugly castle. The town's clean, but there's actually a stink from that place!"

Hmm. Odors of rotting vegetable matter. They forgot to take out the garbage.

They went toward the castle, where there was a booth set up and a play was in progress. Sixty or seventy people were watching the actors. They stopped to watch, for a moment.

There were two actors in robes, standing by a mockup door as though they were about to enter.

"...it therefore wouldst be seemly when we come to those demises that thou wouldst delay thy fork'd tongue.

"But I find that hast its own bewares.

"Be cautious then, bold Fantius, that thy silence doest not betray. The dusty tomes that are bespoken in untimely silence canst far more deadly be than canst words – which canst later be explained in tactful retractions.

"Recall thee, then, that truth which sayest, 'What he hath spoken be only in jest!' wilst change the words that are escap'd of his throat whilst his silence is forever carv'd in bronze.

"A silence canst not be refrain'd from comment, shouldst such silence be more the eloquent reply. If that lack of words be more a speech than is thy comment, then it bespeaks too much, methinks.

"Those who wouldst judge do more far to wisely restrain from their judgments and to allow the silence. Thou doest far wors'd things in the twist'd paths of the gossip's poison'd rantings than couldst imagine in thy dull reality."

The actors opened the door and passed through as another skulked onto the stage with a dagger in his hand.

[There was a great deal of wisdom in those words.]

Yes. It's by a brilliant playwright.

The group went on and into a little pub. "Is the stuff here drinkable?" Z asked.

It's safe, but may be unpalatable. Thing can't drink it. The alcohol is fine, but some of the sugars would be rather extremely unpleasant to it.

The proprietor came to them and bowed low. He was already carrying cups made of pewter and a pewter jug.

He poured them water without looking at them directly.

"What is the fine gentlemen's pleasure?" he asked and looked up into the screen across Tranz's face to see his own face staring back. He dropped the jug.

Z said, "Some of your best wine. Chilled."

The man looked nervous. "I cannot chill the wine, sirs. I have no well."

"Very well. We will chill it," Z replied. "Just bring it, my good man."

The proprietor looked surprised and went for the wine.

"I assume you can chill it?" Z asked.

Yes. I will do a fast heat absorption. Hand the drinks to Thing.

The proprietor came back with four more cups and a large ceramic jug filled with a fair but strong wine. He poured each a cup and Z said, "What is your name?" as he passed the cups to Thing, who waved a tentacle over them and passed them back. The pewter cups quickly formed condensation beads.

"I am called Nettor. Net for short, sirs."

Z said, "Thank you, Net. Leave the jug. We will buy it all."

He waved to Thing and Net handed it the jug. Thing didn't take the jug, but made a couple of passes over it with the tentacle. The jug grew cold in Net's hand.

"Will there be anything else?" Net asked.

"Some sweetcake," Z replied. "Who wrote the play being performed by the castle wall?"

"You *must* be from the far lands," Net said. "It is an old folk play. That is why it is in the old language."

"Oh, we're from far lands," Z replied.

"I can see you and the two other demons are from the far lands." Net sneered. "Your sorcerer would know the play if he were from here."

Net went out a draped door and into the back. He soon returned with hot pastries on a plate.

"I had the wife heat them to save you the trouble," he quipped.

"You would do well to refrain from irritating us," Z said.

"Ha!" Net said. "Do you have any idea how many sorcerers have come to challenge Martin?"

"We didn't come to challenge anyone," Z said. "I assume this Martin is your local wizard?"

"*Local*? No one can be from lands that far!" Net replied, with strange looks for them. "Martin speaks for himself. You do not fool me. I know your sorcerer dares not to speak! Martin will have his tongue!"

"It's not Martin who would have his tongue. He speaks only in a magic tongue and you wouldn't understand him," Z explained.

"But you would?" Net said.

"Of course. Would you care to ask him anything?" Z said.

"Yes," Net replied. "Why does he have no face of his own?"

Z said in Maitan, "Tranz, you will have to speak to me in Maitan. Tom can act insulted that he would dare question the great sorcerer. Thing can moderate in two tongues. All in Maitan. Keep it light. We don't want to make any enemies. Yet."

"Okay," Tranz said, "Tell him I had a fight with my wife and she got my face in the estate settlement."

Tom took out the double bladed knife and ran a finger along the edge.

[We aren't making any real progress here. We can go on to another inn or something.]

I would agree to that.

"We learned the wizard's name," Tranz pointed out.

[That's true.]

"He keeps his face in the castle so it won't be damaged when he goes too close to the sun," Z said.

"Crap! (or at least the equivalent)," Net replied.

While they were talking Thing used a nearly invisible line to drain all the cups and the jug. Net hadn't looked at them, but they hadn't been touched, or he would have noticed.

"We enjoyed the wine," Z said. "It was a quaint little wine with a fair bouquet and a brisk manner. How much do we owe you?"

Net said, "But you didn't...!" He picked up the jug to find it empty. He looked in the cups, which were empty. "Five copens," he said.

Z handed him a gold coin that Maita had minted. It had a picture of Ape on one side and the words "Empire of Maita" in Maitan on the other. It weighed one hundred grams.

Net said, "That's gold! I can't change that!"

"Keep the change," Z said as they went out.

They strolled around for quite awhile, but no one wanted to speak to them, so they went to another pub and had very much the same kind of experience, except this one was more distant with them. As they were leaving, they saw some soldiers in a group, but didn't take much notice until they went back to the clam. There were a ring of soldiers around it and a man in red robes. There were two demons with him. They were trying to open the clam.

I know of those demons! They are from a plane where I once did some work, over a thousand years ago. I'm searching for the language. Yes, I have it. I will translate what I say and what they reply. Stand close to the floater so you can hear.

They moved close to the floater.

Mesorchi! My friends! What are you doing here? It is good to meet good people in strange places!

The demons stopped and came over to Thing, from whom the words seemed to come.

"Who are you who calls us friends?"

I have been to your home world and have worked with the scientists at (schurtziwubble) on the (sensisifoot). It was about eighteen (Frinkls) ago. Gromekt was (Flechtl), at the time.

"Can you aid us? We wish to go home!" one of the Mesorchii cried.

Yes. Come with us in the floater and I will take you home.

"We are guarded here," it answered.

I will handle that. Z, please tell the soldiers and the sorcerer to get out of the way. Tranz, use the wand at lowest power on those who refuse.

Z stepped forward and said, "Get away from our vehicle or we will be forced to take action we wish to avoid."

The sorcerer came forward. He was nervous, watching Tranz out of the corner of his vision.

"You speak the demon tongues?" he asked.

"Seeing as I'm a demon, I suppose you'd have to say that," Z said sarcastically.

"But I mean the demons with me!" the sorcerer said.

Z smirked at him. "But there are no demons with you!" he shot back.

"Those two are under my spell. They cannot escape, as you, a demon, know!" the sorcerer said haughtily.

"They are now with us," Z said. "I'm sure you recognize we are several types of demons here. Don't make the mistake of defying us."

Thing floated over and climbed onto Z's shoulder.

"Eeeee! Your demon has removed its head from its

body!" the sorcerer shouted.

"I would probably know that, as it is now on my shoulders, now wouldn't I?" Z said. "Get away from our vehicle or we will move you ourselves."

The sorcerer stepped aside and waved to the soldiers, who nervously moved toward the group. Tranz stepped forward and looked into the lead soldier's face. The soldier saw himself staring back. He stepped away.

Z said, "We don't wish to harm you. Step aside."

The soldier swallowed hard and stepped to the side. "I ain't gettin' tangled up with no magic!" he protested.

"You will!" the sorcerer said and stepped up to grab the soldier's arm. Tranz touched the sorcerer with the wand and said "Phooey!" The sorcerer was thrown to the ground, where he lay moaning.

"Better him than us," Z said to the soldier and grinned. The soldier grinned back. Tranz held the wand up and the soldiers moved. He went to the clam and it slowly opened.

They got in, bringing the two demons with them. It was a tight fit as the clam closed. They went back to the castle. At the castle Maita asked one of the demons to use the headgear, then left the group at the castle while it took the demons home. When Maita returned, it explained the sorcerers had opened a portal of some sort and had kidnapped various demons, who worked for them in hopes of someday being allowed to return home. None were ever taken home, so far as could be determined, but it was the only chance they had. They were trapped and afraid.

The Mesorchii were actually a good people. It was a pity these sorcerers could do that to them.

[We'll have to do something about that!]

Tomorrow. Get some rest.

In the morning Z awoke and went from the ship to the castle to see what progress the servos were making as to the furnishings. Tom was up on a parapet and waved down to him. He looked up and Tom pointed to the tower opposite. Z looked that way. He saw a large black bird-like being, a Frome, sitting on the wall. Z waved again to Tom, then went quietly up the steep tower stairs. He came out of the door opposite where Tom's tower could be seen and went stealthily around to come up behind the bird. He had placed the language crystal and said very quietly, "Are you from Martin?"

The bird squawked and fell off the wall. It regained its composure and flew up near Z, who waved at it. It flew toward the castle below.

Z went down to the fourth floor hallway, then went to the parapet and leaned over next to Tom to watch the busy servos bustling around below.

"What did you say to it?" Tom asked.

"I told it to say 'hello' to Martin."

"I doubt it's from Martin. Probably some local sorcerer," Tom mused.

"Yeah," Z replied. "Are we going to get to fight some of the demons? I really wouldn't want to fight any of them. They aren't here by choice. Maita says they're really very good people who are afraid and lost here."

Tom grinned. "I'd rather do some of the sorcery stuff," he said. "It would be great fun to have a rivalry with the local practitioners. We have to get hold of some of their books or get one of them on the probe.

"I wonder if any of it's really magic or if its mostly a T.K. power they have."

Z laughed softly and said, "How are we going to tell Maita?

"We can't change any of this, Tom."

Tom replied, "Oh, a little science will end it."

"No!" Z cried. "Tom, I didn't mean we weren't capable of changing it. I meant we can't. Morally. I know we could change it by simply letting them see Maita or an actual floater or anything like that. We can't – *must not* – do that!"

"Why not?" Tom asked.

"Tom, would you take Frezzwin away from your own race's folklore?" Z replied seriously. "I wouldn't take Merlin away from Earth. Not for anything! It would be like taking the heart out of all the kids' fantasies. I wouldn't have wanted to come here at all. I think I'd be a very different person.

"The swords and sorcery and pirates? Would you deprive your kids of those fantasies?"

Tom thought a moment. "Not for life, itself. I see what you mean. I never stopped to think about it before, but you're right."

Z said, "I want to stay here and have some fun. I want to actually live with some of this. We can be a part of the folk tales of this planet for thousands of years. We can maybe selectively change a few things to take some of the ingrained cruelty and brutality out of it, but we'll have to be damned careful. Whether it's a racial fantasy or some being, I think we can make a rivalry where no one gets hurt and everyone builds legends."

Tom shook his head. "This is a hell of a bloody era in a race's history. There are a lot of people who're going to get hurt, and you know it. It's just that sort of a thing."

"But not more than would, anyhow," Z returned quickly. "The only difference'll be that we'll be a part of it. We won't add anything to that. We may be able to stop a little of what would happen along the more negative lines. That's the sort of thing I want to do."

They saw Thing come out of the ship and look around. It saw them and drifted up to join them.

[Hi, guys! The castle's coming along very well, I think. Maita wants us to come in later to discuss all this. It says none of it's necessary. We can end this quickly and get away, but it knows you want to make a kind of vacation out of it. Maita wants to study these people awhile, too. I find them to be surprising, in a lot of ways. They are a strange race. We can put an end to the sorcery and stay to study the people for a certain time.]

"No!" Tom and Z shouted together.

[I don't understand!]

Z explained, "Thing, this is an important time. We can't interfere."

[I sort of thought we had no business here. I feel we are in a moral dilemma, and should go. I don't know if you can make Maita see, though. It's very interested in what kind of psy powers the sorcerers have. The general populace doesn't exhibit it, but the magicians must have something such to be able to call the Fromes and other demons. Maita wants to find parallels with the transmats and the psy.]

Tom said, "If we have to, we'll outvote Maita. We musn't interfere, but that doesn't mean we have to leave. I want to stay awhile. So does Z."

[Why?]

Z took Thing off the floater to sit it on his shoulder.

"It's a fantasy Tom and I want to live inside of, for a bit," he explained.

[What are we going to do? I will help. I can sense this is important to you.]

"We'll go to the meeting," Tom replied. "Maita understands more of this than you know."

They went back to the ship and into room two.

Good morning, all! I heard your discussion through Thing's floater. I don't mean to eavesdrop, but if I'm to translate for Thing, I must know what's said.

"We don't mind, Maita," Tom said. "We do want to make you understand, though. We can't interfere here."

I understood why this is so important to you racially when you said Triss would have the same legends. It's part of the racial evolution. It's very possibly impressed from outside, you know. That makes it artificial, and not really necessary.

Z said, "Maita? Please listen carefully. Listen to what I mean. I'm not too sure I can express what I feel well. It's a very complicated thing.

"I guess I can say that ... no. If you check, you'll find that races like the Immins have no such past legends. The race has a severe lack, as a result. The Immins are very practical. They are logical in their own way. They are, therefore, innately evil. You know that.

"I'm not saying this well! I can't find the right words!

"The Immins have no magic, though they'll fear it. I know this will prove true, though I know next to nothing about them. The Bentans won't have these legends. The Trath won't have the legends, but the Cheeth will! Do you have any idea what I'm saying?"

[I do. None of those races – except the Cheeth – have any sense of wonder about them. They progress when it's thrust upon them, not from curiosity. We've given the Trath a small moral legend that might save them and the Bentans are all right. They have other strengths. The Cheeth are really quite a fine people.]

*Yes. I think you are saying some being is going around

the galaxy teaching them to wonder and to be curious. They can have knowledge, therefore control of their world and later of the universe, if they try. It's a reason to outreach their limits. And I'm not expressing myself any better than you are. We do understand one another.*

Tom said, "I think you have it very closely to the truth.

"Did the Maitans have this legend?"

That would be over three hundred thousands of years ago. Let me regress.

Maita was silent for several minutes, during which Tranz came into the room and sat, after pouring himself a cup of gincha. He looked a question at Tom, who shook his head.

The silence lasted a bit longer.

Yes. They had a story of a poor youth who went into an enchanted mountain, where he found a large ruby embedded into the rock face of a cliff. There was a fire inside the ruby that would answer the boy's questions if he held it in his hands. Only the chosen one could take the ruby from the rock. It fell into the hands of the youth, known as Tamm. Tamm became the greatest king Maita has ever known. He gave them such things as medicine and metal working. All of this had been predicted by a magician, Arbettin.

[Yes. It had to be. Do you realize how old this magician would have to be?]

Z grinned. "Oh, only a few million years," he answered.

Tom insisted, "We can't interfere."

I agree. We will remove this castle and go.

[No, Maita.]

Why not?

[We can go. You can go. I can go. Tranz can go. Z and Tom will remain. They have better sense than to interfere with things, but it's a chance for them to live in a fantasy. It's the past – things as they were. They can learn. We have no right to deprive them of anything.]

Tranz said, "I agree. I don't belong here. My race has legends of a different type altogether, but we have the legends. Perhaps I fear to meet who or what is planting these things in all our races.

"I wish to return to Empire Center. I don't wish to ask anyone else to leave here."

[I wish to remain with you. I plead that I will follow your instructions, exactly. I can learn so much that isn't available to be learned elsewhere or by any other method. This is like a special educational project for me. I am interested in any strange mental ability.]

I wish to remain, solely as an observer. I will take no part, unless asked. This is a decision of Tom and Z. I also think it will be as much fun as Z says!

Z said, "I'll be glad to have all of you. We really can have a lot of fun, but it's also tremendously dangerous. It's completely serious on one level, but that doesn't mean we can't enjoy it on another. I think we should be the light and funny type to counter the bloodiness of the time."

Tom nodded agreement. He added, "We'll be glad for Tranz to stay, but I know what he means about fearing to meet someone who made my entire race what it is. I'm torn, but I wouldn't go for anything! If all of you want to go, I'll stay on my own!"

"I plead cowardice, pure and simple," Tranz said. "I'm terrified of meeting this creature face to face. It would be too much like meeting god.

"I wish to go. I'm sorry if it causes inconvenience. I'm sorry. You could perhaps drop me at Fortney if it'll save time or anything."

[There's no inconvenience. Maita will energize the portal and you will step out in the caves.]

"Will the portal work at this distance?" Tranz asked.

It works at any distance. The mental stuff will only work for eight plazsis, but our system will work anywhere in the galaxy. The interface is everywhere. If there is such a portal — Great exploding galaxies! If there's another portal in the farthest galaxy from here that's tuned exactly like ours, someone could step through to our portal! Wow!

"I hope none of you will feel less of me for leaving," Tranz said. "If there's any emergency where you need me, call me and open the portal and I'll be here. I think you know that."

Tranz went back to Empire Center and the rest went to the pilot's dome.

*It's your show. Tell us what you want. I didn't want to say anything while Tranz was still here, but I'm a little scared about that portal, now. It really *could* bring some-one from another galaxy. I have to study this. Thing will too. What should I do here?*

[I think galactic drift factors make it unlikely anyone could travel between galaxies with the portals.]

"Rig a reading helmet on the floater under Thing," Tom said. "We're going to have to read how the sorcerers do the magic stuff."

Now wait! I didn't say I'd break my own code!

Z laughed and said, "We'll work it so the sorcerer never knows he was read. Some of them have found ways to directly read others with whatever psy talents they have. It's nothing to them, so why should we worry? You might also bear in mind they're calling beings from other planes and are using them as slaves, so they don't deserve any such rights, anyhow!"

[How could they do that? Read others directly?]

"I think it's a talent the — whatever level it is — mind suppresses, probably for good reason," Tom answered. "I would think our builders of the Tristar never had the legends as their talents developed. They weren't evil. As a matter of fact they were reaching out, in their own way, to invite all others to join them on EC. That was the purpose of the three different colored stars. It was to say, 'Here we are. Come to us.'

"Don't your own communicators directly read other beings who don't have the empathic abilities? Maybe this being or whatever knows the danger of racial destruction from the talent."

[It's certainly latent in you. We discovered that on EC, if nothing else! (Book four: *Tristar*)]

What do we do? Our sorcerer's gone. We're a weird collection of odd demons, now.

Tom said, "I look more like a demon than Z. Z can be a normal person of a far land, as well as a wizard. I'll be a demon, as will Thing. Z's the boss, so we do what he says. That will give the local wizard someone to focus his worst challenges on – and it won't be me!"

"You can make a golem!" Z suddenly cried. "A good wizard has a golem! Apollonius of Tyanna traveled to Tibet and told of golem heads made of bronze that could speak and often prophetize. I'm such a powerful wizard I fooled them into thinking a simple projection was the wizard! I'm also so powerful I taught all the people in my entourage the language – even the golem heads.

"Part of the fun will be that we'll have three, no, only two heads on the golem. They'll be mounted on a plate floater, facing in opposite directions. They can't see each other. They'll look almost identical. Make a few superficial differences in them. One can be sour-looking and one can look pious. They'll be our prophet familiars, one of doom and one overly optimistic. They'll get into arguments with each other that only I can stop. They'll seem to always be trying to drive us nuts, bickering like spoiled brats!

"What they say must have some lessons and meanings, but they can also be pains in the ass!

"I'll need a lot of props if I'm to impress anyone I should get to know Martin face to face.

"I'll admit I'm scared shitless to meet whatever it is, too. Tranz might be the smartest one of us to get the hell out."

They went to the hold to use the holo tank to design the heads Maita made out of bronze. They had mouths that worked well, with hinged lips. The hinges were hidden, so they looked almost natural, unless one was close and could see the seams. The eyes were emeralds and rubies, back-to-back. A back light could make them change, according to mood. They simply turned in the sockets.

They were the normal size of heads among the Tlorgians, and had the same general features. The pious head would have a whiny voice while the other would snarl.

Tom suggested, "The heads should give advice and join into conversations – interrupt into conversations would be a better way to describe it. Use one with higher tones and voice and Thing can be ... no. Thing will have to use its own voice. You can use some other for the second head. Use your own for one so we can communicate if we have to with others around. Maitan will be the 'Magicians language' we use to chat among ourselves."

"Use Ape's voice for the other," Z said.

They made the golem heads and Maita tested them, giving the negative head a different tone than had been used for Ape. It was a bit acid in tone. (– will be used to denote No, the negative head, as * is used for Maita.)

I say that today will be sunny and cool.

–You! You say! You say! Can't you see the thunder clouds are gathering? You fool! It's going to rain and ruin my finish. How can you *always* be so stupid? Why don't you ever shut the hells up? You're such an idiot!–

You should drop dead! Can't you see the clouds are too far away to bother us? It will be a fine day.

–If we have a cyclone, you'd say it will clear up soon. Idiot! Life isn't all gold and silver! Stupid! You've made moronics into a branch of science! You've made stupid an art form!–

You really should try to see that life isn't all lead, either. The day will be very nice. It will be sunny, with a light breeze. Try to look on the bright side of these things and life will be so much more pleasant for us all!

–You make me so mad with all that sweetness and warmth! How can you be so unrealistic? Dolt!–

I wish you'd take the time to....

"Knock it off!" Z yelled.

You said only you could make me stop.

[Out there. Not here.]

Are you going to turn into a critic?

"It always was," Tom said.

[But then, you have a lot to criticize.]

–And I suppose you don't?–

Who asked you, Bronze Brain?

–You're supposed to be the nice one.–

[Gheesh! I always knew you would end up in a sick claw-fight with yourself.]

"My God!" Z cried. "How did all this start? Recheck your circuits, Maita. Something's burned out."

[You're the one who's burned out, though I don't know how you managed it. All your circuits seem to be locked on standby, most of the time.]

"Yeah? And all yours are on sitby," Z countered.

"That was pretty good," Tom said.

How would you know? Yours are turned off.

–There you go again, Ammonia Breath. You're supposed

to be the nice one.–

Oh yeah. I can't seem to keep that straight.

"Enough!" Z cried. "It works beautifully. Don't use all your lines now. I know you have a limited number of ideas."

–It's better than no ideas at all!–

"You're my idea, Metal Mouth!" Z returned.

[Metal mouth? Is that the best you can do?]

"I'm going to save my better replies for a more discerning audience," Z sniffed haughtily.

[Well, if that's an example of the best I certainly don't want to hear the better.]

"That's pretty good!" Tom put in. "For a lump of Silly Putty."

[Go chase your tail. Preferably one meter outside of the upper rampart.]

They kept the banter up awhile, then went back to their own quarters to clean up and eat. They were to go back to town that night to try to get a sorcerer onto the headgear.

They waited until sunset, climbed into the clam, and again parked by the fountain, then went immediately into Net's pub, where they sat at the same table as the night before. Net came to the table and said, "Where's your wizard? You don't think I'm going to serve unaccompanied demons do you?"

Z smiled at him. "I've got some news for you, pal. I'm the wizard. The one last night was only a projection.

"Bring us some wine and sweetcake. The golems won't be dining."

Net looked at the heads. "I wouldn't imagine," he said.

–When you uncork the wine you can place the cork in your ugly face, Smiley. Maybe bring two bottles and shove the other cork up your ass!–

Don't be so unkind. He couldn't tell the cook our orders, that way. I could suggest a more pleasant demeanor among all of us. Dining is so much pleasanter if there isn't all this silly contention.

–Why don't you weld your lips together, Dung Breath?–

"You two stop it," Z said. "Please don't make them argue again, Net. They give me a headache."

"They give me a lower pain," Tom said.

[You're doing it wrong!]

"Knock it off!" Z said.

Net stared a second at them, then walked back toward the kitchen.

"What was that you said, Thing?" Tom asked.

"It's an old joke from Earth," Z said. "A man and his wife went to a marriage counselor because they thought their lives were empty and they were missing something. The counselor asked them questions about their lives together. When he asked the wife what their sex life was like she said, 'Sex is nothing but a pain in the butt!'

"The doctor replied, 'You're doing it wrong.'"

Tom started giggling, and was still at it when Net returned with the wine. "Did I miss something?" he asked.

[About ninety percent of what's said, but you can't help it that your head is so low.]

Net put the wine and sweetcakes down with the tray and walked off, leaving them to serve themselves. Z tasted the wine and said, "Not bad. A little strong."

He tried the sweetcake and remarked that it was a little bitter.

Put some on the floater.

Z put a bit on the floater and Maita said, *It's laced with a strong alkaloid poison. If your system was more like the Tlorgians you'd be dead in a very short time. Use the antidote on the floater.*

Z took the pill and called Net over. "Bring more of these sweetcakes. They're very good! What's the strange spice that gives them that extra tang?"

Net looked a moment and went back to the kitchen. He returned a moment later with a large platter of the sweetcakes. Z tasted one. It was more bitter than the last.

"Sit down with us, Net," he said as he ate one of the cakes and picked up another.

Net became nervous. "I've got other customers."

"Where?" Z asked. "Sit."

Net sat and Z handed him a sweetcake. "These are actually very good. Eat one."

"I can't have sweets," Net whined.

Tom smiled a very fangy smile. "Eat one," he said. "One can't hurt."

–Hee hee! Force-feed the son of a frumpt.–

Don't be so bloodthirsty. The poison will kill him! That would be unconscionable!

–So what, Demon Dome? That's what it's supposed to do to Boss.–

It can't hurt Boss. Boss is a wizard. He's immune.

–He's not immune to wanting revenge, Airdome.–

You should be more understanding. Someone made him put the poison in the cakes, didn't they, Net?

–Why don't you see if the furnace is hot enough to cast a new statue? You could sit in there for awhile, just to make sure.–

"You two stop it!" Z demanded. "I asked you not to do anything to get them started, Net.

"Who had you put the poison in the cakes?"

He ate another and Maita told him not to eat anymore. In Maitan.

"He'll turn me into something nasty if I tell you!" Net cried.

[Then tell us if we are wrong. Was it the sorcerer who tried to get into our, uh, clam last night?]

Net stared at the table.

Tom asked, "Was it Martin?"

"No! Martin had nothing to do with it. He wouldn't resort to anything like that! Martin would *never* do anything like that!" Net was outraged because of the mention of this sort of thing with Martin?

"Oh. Then it must have been last night's sorcerer?" Tom asked.

Net stared at the table.

Z said, "Well, if you won't tell us, you won't tell us.

"Let's go."

He stood and put another of the gold coins on the table.

"Thank you," Net said as they left.

They went back to the platform where the play was being performed as it was last night. It was later in the play, and was being acted on a different stage.

The night before they noticed there were three stages. The action they had seen was the center stage while the ones on either side had curtains dropped across them. The action now was in the right stage, which was shown as a room with several actors in it. Three were seated, while the one referred to as Fantius last evening was standing to make a speech. The center stage was open to the audience, and the one who had been approaching with the knife was communicating with another dressed in sorcerer's robes in the center stage area.

Very clever. It allows the audience to see the plotters as well as the present action. It also saves the time it would take to change the sets.

Fantius was speaking: "Wouldst that I were but half of thy vile accusations! Should there be man with prowess to accomplish such deeds, wouldst come to this place?

Wouldst allow such questionings?

"Methinks not!

"Had this one man the power or the influence thy sly inferences accuse, wouldst have thou courage to utter these words?

"Methinks not!

"No my lords! Methinks not!

"Thou art as the pett'd animals which are paint'd and comb'd for thy mistresses to parade upon yon square. Thou art, each, own'd and property of thy masters.

"Thy time is short.

"Delay then here and await the twistings of thy deaths. Thou wilst halt me not one step! Thou hast not courage enow!

"Come, Listus. We depart this sick'ning company to yon baths. I feeleth unclean. Leave the pett'd animals for their whores to parade in yon square whilst around the feet of their whores falleth the decay of their empires! Let us begone from this stink of moral corruption!"

The two actors stepped through the door and onto the center stage.

Listus: "Ah! My good Fantius, methinks thou hast become undone. Thy words may afright those unworthies in their dens, but aforelong do those consider thy concepts and strike!

"Wouldst be away!"

The actor in the sorcerer's robes stepped to them and they cowered back against the door. The hood was thrown back and the sorcerer was shown to be an adolescent boy.

Fantius: "Tis but young Martin! Thou didst give us much afright, young lad! Thou art surely growing of stature!"

Martin: "Heed then these words!

"The child of thy loins, Fantius, known as Cleethy the Beautiful, shall have unto her a son.

"The child of thy loins, Listus, known as Farro the Bold, shall be sire of this child.

"The child wilst be known forevermore. He shall be nam'd Clestius, and wilst be king emperor of all the lands of Tlorg wherein dwell civilized men.

"Ye shall know the prophesy is fulfil'd whence the age of the child be twelve years. For I say unto you the child of thy children wilst remove the Lock of Thorus from the Well of Hope and wilst deliver his people from slavery under the whoremasters of Tlorg!

"This be my prophesy, for I have seen what be to come.

"Go ye forward in peace. The whoremasters inside wilst not this night survive."

The actors were showing shock as the curtains fell.

[I wonder if that's the same Martin who's the great wizard here? It would seem to have to be the case.]

Tom said, "I'm sure it is. There wouldn't be two of them."

But if the play's really folklore, how old is it?

Z said, "It may be a couple of years old and brought from 'somewhere' as folklore, or it may be centuries old."

These people don't live centuries.

"Neither do Earth people," Z said. "Apollonius of Tyana was seen regularly for three hundred years."

"Yeah. Frezwin lived for half a millennium on Zeena, according to the records," Tom added.

[We must get a sorcerer onto the machine.]

"And a historian," Tom said.

They left as the left curtain was going up on the third stage, showing a stone well with a large bronze lock holding a stone lid on it.

There were soldiers around the clam again – with the sorcerer from the night before. Z went up to the sorcerer, who was trying various chants on the clam. He was about to speak when the clam started to open.

He waited a moment. The clam opened a few inches, then dropped closed again.

A soldier thrust a bronze sword blade into the opening and pried upward. He was a powerful man and the sword bent. He looked up to see Z watching him and made a squealing sound.

Z grinned and shook his head. The wizard spun around, fear on his face, along with the surprise.

Z grinned and said, "I can't be poisoned. Net didn't tell me who you were but, as the play there says, his silence spoke dusty tomes.

"If you want to see inside of our clam all you have to do is ask."

Z turned to the clam and said, "Open sesame!" and the top sprang open.

"It's a matter of speaking the correct incantation," Z explained. "I think you were as close as you ever would've gotten.

"Get in."

"I merely wanted to see!" the sorcerer cried.

Tom said, "So, you saw. Get in and we'll take you for a ride."

"I wouldn't think of taking your valuable time," the sorcerer whined.

"Oh, our time isn't valuable," Z replied. "We're mostly wastrels and loafers. We'll take you for a ride up to our castle. I'm sure you'll love the place! It's made of gold, you know – No, no! We insist!"

He fingered the wand Tranz had used on the sorcerer the night before. The sorcerer looked very shaky and not a little sick.

"Well, if it isn't too much trouble," he muttered.

*We will be most happy to give you a ride. It's a very

pleasant form of conveyance I'm sure you will enjoy. The ride is both smooth and quiet, so one may collect one's thoughts to contemplate the marvels of nature in serene and pleasant surroundings.*

–Oh, shut up, Mealy Mouth! He'll probably get so nervous he'll puke all over it! Why are you so damned stupid?–

That is a most unkind thing to say. You are always so negative about everything. Don't ruin a very nice ride for everyone else with your negative attitude! Be nice!

–Stick it in your nose, Bubble Brain!–

[Stop it! He's our guest!]

–I don't remember asking you, Stretch Mouth.–

Don't be so unkind to people. Mainly, remember that Rubber Brain there has certain powers.

–I'm so scared I could go to sleep.–

[Cool off.] Thing said and made a pass over the negative head. Ice formed on it.

I tried to warn you. You never listen!

–B b brr uh uh brr+–

"Stop it!" Z demanded. "I apologize. They're sometimes very hard to control.

"I'm called Boss, the black demon is Extrx, the golem with the ice is No and the other one is Yes. Maybe's the one who did the cute little trick with the temperature of the No head."

Z poured a goblet of wine and held it against No to cool it. "*That* trick, I'll have to remember, No. You'll stay cold a lot longer than a little ice. Good trick, Maybe!" He turned to the sorcerer, who was staring in obvious fear and confusion.

"What are you called?" Tom asked.

The sorcerer said, "They call me Tee."

"That's easy to remember," Z said. "It's not your name,

of course. Your name is...."

Maita used the instant sedation and Thing put the helmet on Tee's head. After about five minutes, Maita gave Z the name and said, *Three, two, one, now.*

"...Wellor Sczim Fornesh Cromin, but we'll all pretend I don't know, if it makes you uneasy that I *do* know.

"We are here."

They landed on the parapet by a tower and the clam top opened. They got out, Tee none too steadily. Z leaned against the wall and looked toward the town, which showed nicely in the many torch lights.

"Rather pretty," he said and went into the tower. The rest of them followed. There was nothing inside the tower but an inlaid marble floor. No other doors, except one going to the rampart on the other side of the tower.

Down.

The floor began descending with the group on it.

–Why don't you just wait until you're told before you start giving orders to the demons? One of these days you'll get us both killed! What if Gembozzle decides he's had enough of your arrogant attitude, Vacuum Brain?–

It was obvious we would be descending. We were all on the floor. Please try to be nice.

–I got news for you, Malachite Mind, you can't see this side.–

"You two stop it," Z said.

They were in the bottom of the tower, where a bronze door had been exposed. Z opened it and they stepped into a magnificent hall with a table full of fruits and steaming dishes. There were several varieties of wines.

"How does that tower thing work?" Tee asked. "This is the most unbelievable place I have ever seen! How can the temperature be so comfortable without fires at this altitude? Is that food all real? It smells so good! What are those red jewels on the tableware? How do you get such a shine on the silver? Is that real gold?"

[Everything is real. We may be wastrels and loafers, but we enjoy the finer things in life. It's nice to have enough power to call up about anything we could want.]

"Anything?" Tee asked, greed almost dripping off him.

Z smiled and said, "Within reason. It would be stupid to say I wanted all the diamonds in the world in this room. I would be neck deep in diamonds. I could say I wanted the largest flawless diamond in this world and get it, though."

"Really?" Tee asked, greed positively dripping from him a bit more.

Z waved a hand lazily and said, "Oh, Troonah. Ibbldey piggledy and snake in the grass. Put a big diamond on a floater and send it fast," in Maitan.

[And Z can then shove it up his silly ass!]

Tom giggled.

Tee looked expectant.

"It will take a couple of minutes. Troonah has to send Ibbledy and Piggledy out to search the whole world," Z said carelessly. "Ah, here it is!"

A floater came in with a diamond about six inches thick on it.

"The least you could have done is cut and polished it, Troonah," Tom chided.

There was a fog around the diamond for a few seconds. It dissipated to reveal the huge diamond, now cut into hundreds of flashing facets.

"Troonah gets lazy if you don't keep right on top of him," Tom said. "Some of these demons – Boss is usually too easy on them!"

"What a diamond!" Tee cried. "Great Martin! I didn't think there was any diamond half so large! Why, it must weigh several kilos!"

Z waved a hand and said, "It's yours. What?"

He acted as though he were listening a moment. "Oh. Sorry Tee. I can't give it to anyone not accepted in the guild. You know the rules."

"What guild?" Tee asked.

"I can't tell you. If you qualify, you'll know," Z said. "Eat, drink! We don't poison things. It ruins the flavor."

[If he qualified he would be able to have Troonah bring him the thing.]

After about a half hour of showing the sorcerer around and listening to him try to get them to give him jewels or a method to get his own they had the floater take him back and drop him off at the fountain.

I have a crystal of all he knows about sorcery. It really is amazing! I wasn't opening the clam. It was the spells. I didn't believe that stuff really worked!

Tom said, "We told you some of the powers are real. You'll have to be careful. It could probably damage you in some way you don't expect.

"I want to know how old that play is."

From what Tee knows, it's at least four hundred years old. We will have to get a historian.

Z took the crystal from the floater and placed it in the socket. Tom took the other.

Z spun and threw a spark off the end of his finger that caught Tom on the tail. Tom jumped and yelled, "Ow!"

Tom threw a bolt of light at Z, who ducked. "Hold it a minute," Tom said. "I forgot I'm sensitive. That bolt could have hurt you."

"I think I could defense it," Z replied. "It was mostly light, so I shielded my eyes."

Are you two actually using magic?

"Yeah," Tom replied. "Watch!"

He stood in the middle of the room and went invisible.

"See?" he said. "That was the inertia field. Somethin' else, huh?

"This is as good as I can do, and it's already fading. It'll give you an idea of the power Martin has if he can hide a whole planet for weeks."

I'm beginning to respect this stuff. I don't see how you can do it!

Thing disappeared.

I figured you could do it, if Tom could.

[Oh, I didn't use an inertia field.] Thing came in from the next room. [I wanted to try to teleport. It's both an amazing and unexpected experience – and very scary.]

Tom said, "I see it worked. I'll try."

[No!]

"Why not?" Tom asked, pausing.

[I was only going to teleport a bit behind Z. I went in another direction and was within inches of being inside a solid wall. I think they don't use it because it's not controllable. You can see the warnings that are in Tee's mind. It would be a good idea to beware. We have to follow those warnings!]

Z studied the thought. "Whew! Didn't you see that bit, Thing?"

[Yes, but I was stupid enough to think I could handle it, despite the warnings. I know better, now. I won't be so stupidly arrogant about my abilities in the future, I can guarantee! If I had materialized – that's not what happens, but it will have to do – inside of an occupied space with any really dense material there, I could have become a small nova machine.]

Nova machine? That's a dephased moder.

"It causes two objects to occupy the same space on an atomic level," Z said. "The same thing could happen. It's not likely, but it's not impossible, either."

"Let's make a strict rule we don't experiment with things past the warnings," Tom suggested. "They're there for a very good reason."

[I agree.]

"So do I," Z said.

It doesn't matter to me. Only an organic mind could use most of it.

Tee was furious and confused. This foreign sorcerer had taken two of his demons and had returned them to the demonland! That was not done! Not ever! It was a direct challenge!

Those demons were his source of power. Now he had only two left, and was a bit afraid of setting up the power construct and energizing it again, because Martin had decreed there were to be no more callings.

Martin hadn't been here in years! He would probably never return, but that was a chance no one could afford to take. Martin didn't use any trickery and he didn't have a sense of humor when it came to other sorcerers.

Tee didn't doubt for a single second Martin had the power to crush him if he too openly defied any of the decrees. Stealth was important. Holding this kind of power was dangerous for reasons of its own, much less for the fact Martin would destroy him if he was exposed too soon. He must become strong enough that even Martin wouldn't defy him.

These strange demons and this sorcerer were not using forbidden powers, so they must fear Martin as he did. They had that much intelligence, if they didn't have enough to realize the sorcerer Tee had far more power than he put on display for such as they!

That pure gold castle! It was real, not an illusion. Tee was there. He used every counterspell he knew to expose the trickery or spells used to give illusion. The castle was exactly as it seemed. Those ever-full tables held real food, too. He had filled his pockets and had tested it all after he got back to the Count's castle. The delicacies and fine wines were beyond price. Few would ever have even a part of those foods in a lifetime.

That clam shell was another thing, altogether. That it did work wasn't questionable in any way – but how? There was no spell on it! Where did it get its levitation without a spell? Why could it resist the strongest spells he could call up to open it? Where did the light come from? How did they get all those little squares of ice up there in that castle? Why didn't they melt, in this heat? How could they keep the wine so cool?

He was glad they hadn't noticed his fear in the craft. He was sure he had fainted for a second or two, but only he was aware of that. Any display of that kind of weakness could and would destroy him in the conflict that surely must come – and soon!

Tee took another large volume from the shelf and opened it to energy spells. It was surely going to come to having to challenge this foreigner or abdicating his power over this entire area.

He had surpassed the wizard at Forthern Castle, who was the only challenger in this whole part of the kingdom. Once Teeme was solidly under his power, he could think of extending even to Loosta itself.

King Wizard Tee!

There was a definite challenge from that wizard and his demons. It would come to a duel to the death. It was ever closer to the challenge.

It was coming.

<u>*Reasons*</u>

The next morning Thing and Z were on the parapet, looking down on the village and enjoying the chilling breeze blowing in from the plains. Tom had gone to the far side of the high mountains on a floater just to "see what was over there."

[Z, what are you going to do when you run up against the inevitable fact that your fun and games are getting you in deeper than you can possibly ever hope to extricate yourself from, even if you live to be ten billion years old, and are on this planet when this area of the galaxy becomes energy-poor to the extent that you couldn't boil an egg on the surface of any sun between here and galactic center?]

"For Christ's sake, Thing!" Z exploded. "Please don't use such long sentences. I'm out of breath from listening to you."

[What? The machine can handle any length sentence I feed it.]

"That's not the point."

[What is?]

"I forgot what you asked."

[So did I.]

Thing asked you what....

[Never mind.]

"Never mind."

Well, we have to figure where we go from here. Thing, we agreed not to interfere with what they do, so let them make as big fools of themselves as they please.

"We have to wait. Martin will come to us." Z seemed positive.

Tom flew up on the floater. "Not even maybe," he said.

"Why not?" from Z.

"Well, why should he?" Tom asked. "If the situation were reversed, would you come here?"

"Sure!" Z said. "I'd have to see what was going on. I'd have to know who the usurpers were and how they got the power to do all we've done here."

If that thing's a power that has been moving around the galaxy for a few million years it knows damned well how much power we have and how far we could possibly go toward causing it trouble. If this magic used by such little petty magicians as Tee can do the things you have demonstrated this Martin has a few powers beyond my comprehension. His ability to make that null inertia field larger than this planet shows how far you will be allowed to go!

"Not far," Tom agreed. "It can cut us off at any time.

"I think it'll enjoy the challenge. We may be fun for it. I think it would get unbelievably bored if it's been around for the past five hundred thousand years or so."

[Then why does it continue?]

"Because it feels responsible," Z replied. "It's either a god, or it's become as much as one.

"Remember how the Ithians of Kroon said any gods were totally irrelevant? (Book two: *Settling In*) I rather doubt they'd say that about whoever or whatever is here!"

[Now I am getting fearful.]

"It's steering thousands of races," Tom said. "Think of it. Tranz said his race has legends of the type, but not the same ones. He's a reptile, so would be different. Even his race has the benefits of this being – or these beings, as the case may be. I want to ask it how it selects which races it'll help."

Well, what are you going to do next? Philosophize?

"We've got to do something to get Martin's attention," Z

insisted. "We can go to town around noon and be visible. Maybe do a bit of the magic stuff or heal somebody or something. Show him we're not like this Tee character. We can show him that we *do* have *some* few redeeming characteristics!"

"I think that would probably be far the quickest way to get Martin's attention," Tom agreed. "We can be healers. This guy seems to want to help the races, so maybe he'll notice if we do the same."

[That doesn't logically follow. He may do all this simply to see what happens. The ones who don't seem to get his attentions are his control group. It may be some kind of scientific study by a being who really *is* immortal.]

On the other hand, he may actually be trying to help. We will have to remember to ask him.

"Save the sarcasm for No," Tom said. "Let's go to town. I saw a bunch of riders come in from the mountains a little after dawn, so I'd like to find out what's happening down there. I wonder if maybe we aren't the focus of attention. I wonder if they're mercenaries.

"They rode through the town and directly to the castle."

Z said, "I think we should call on the fancy castle to introduce ourselves. What little I've heard about the people in the castle shows me they leave a whole lot to be desired as leaders of anything. If they've called in mercenaries to handle us, I'd like to be a step or three ahead of them."

I have a suggestion.

They waited. Finally Tom said, "Well?"

Do you want to hear it? I agreed not to get involved.

Z said, "We want you involved. What's the idea?"

As you will remember, when we were on Earth how a Chinese girl went on the probe machine to teach us the languages we didn't know from you, Z.

"Yes?" Z asked.

She was an expert in hand-to-hand combat and martial arts, as well as an excellent fencing competitor. I can put those arts on a crystal and you can use it on the open sockets. It may come in rather handy because these people aren't physiologically too greatly different from you two.

Tom said, "That would be great! I know how to use a knife, but the sword's for decoration. They fight with swords here, so it would be a good idea to be able to defend myself with one. The hand-to-hand bit could be very useful, also. If what once happened on Zeena's anything like the same schedule here, fencing won't be around for another couple of hundred years. We could make their best swordsmen look silly and ineffective."

Z agreed and Maita produced the crystals. Both Tom and Z placed them in the secondary sockets.

"Shall we go to town?" Z asked.

Tom said, "The clam's great for evening wear, but I think we should use something different in the daytime. We don't want to be out of style. Loafers and wastrels seldom are."

What do you suggest?

They thought awhile. Finally, Z suggested, "I've got it! A flying carpet! It can be a richly woven mural-tapestry sort of thing. You see tapestries around. They seem to be a sign of wealth.

"We wouldn't want to overdo the vast wealth bit (snigger), but one must be ostentatious when one *is* being ostentatious!

"How much mass will one of those small antigravity discs manage?"

A bit more than a kilogram.

"You can weave them all through the carpet and can put a circuit in so we can turn them up, down or off. Sort of a rheostat thing," Z suggested. "One of the one-meter floaters can be made to look like a small table in the center of the rug and we'll sit around it, drinking fine wines. It'll give us directional flight while the discs give us lift. That'll let the carpet wave and fold."

[Maita can use a fine material and make the table a hollow tube that we can fold the tapestry into when we get off. Z can then 'order' the container to go to the top of a tree or to just hover above reach until we need it again. He can then make an incantation and it will come.]

Tom said, "It can automatically fold itself when we get off and automatically unfold when we want to get back on."

Tom wanted to make the design only the power symbol, but Z wanted to have the castle on it with the symbol at all four corners. The castle could be in pure gold thread. They opted for that, because the weavers of tapestries would know it would take years to weave that design, while the castle had only been there a few days. They added all the power symbols they could discover from the sorcerer's crystal and what they had seen.

Their own symbol was larger, of course.

They made the carpet and tested it, then flew into the town. They stopped at the fountain, where all the riders who came in that morning were assembled. The riders were dirty, wearing gaudy costumes and carrying all the weapons they could carry. They were in excellent physical shape, though some were wounded in various ways. The mounts, a somewhat camel-like animal, were hung with rugs and larger weapons.

The crew dismounted and Z waved the carpet into the tube and to about thirty meters above the fountain, where it hovered. The group turned to look at the riders, who stared back in open hostility. One of the riders had a badly infected wound on his arm. He was feverish, weak and on the verge of falling off his mount. Z looked as concerned as he knew to look and approached the rider. The other riders tensed.

"Maita," Z said in Maitan, "Make me a batch of penicillin or something like that. Sulfathiamazol."

It would kill him. Anaphylactic rejection.

"Tetracycline?"

Oxytetracycline. It will work fast. Their systems can handle it.

Z said in Tlorg, "Dismount and I'll give you something to cure your infections."

Another rider spoke in an odd dialect, which the crystal immediately identified.

"I'm sorry," Z replied – in that language. "I'm used to Loostan. I should speak Verfral.

"Please dismount and I'll give you something to cure your wounds. That infection looks very serious."

The other riders muttered about the fact Z spoke without accent. The golem heads went into their act – in Verfral.

–There you go with your goody-goody stupidity. You don't show any sense at all, for the world's greatest wizard. This forest vermin won't appreciate it. Let him die!–

*Why, *why* are you always so anxious to belittle others? These people have done you no wrong. Be nice! Try to show a little compassion to these less fortunate beings.*

–Shut up, Verdigris Head! I didn't ask you! You drive me crazy! Sheesh!–

Please be a little considerate of others. It is such a nice day. Why spoil it?

–What nice day? Idiot! We have to wake up and come out here so our fearless leader can play physician? When was I elected to be a nurse to a bunch of savages? Drop dead already!–

"Stop it!" Z ordered.

The riders were staring at the heads as the rider Z was addressing's eyes rolled up and he began to slide off the mount. He came to and caught himself.

Tom said, "You're dying. Don't be a fool. Boss can help you. Get off the damned mount and let him do something."

The rider shook his head to try to clear it. He slowly dismounted and stood shakily. "I make no bargain for my soul, sorcerer," he mumbled.

Z smiled and said, "I'm not a sorcerer. I'm a wizard. I make no bargains. I'll heal you and don't care if I never see or hear of you again. I've known much pain. I don't enjoy seeing it in others. It reminds me."

He turned to the floater with the heads, where there were some pills and a gold jar of salve. He cut the dirty bandages off the arm and was confronted with a festering, stinking, ugly sore and a deep infected gash.

He spoke in Maitan. "Maita, this is gangrenous. It's too far gone. I don't think he'll live. We've made a big mistake here. If this man dies after we said we'd save him, we lose face for all time!"

The salve contains some Bacitracin and a strong anti-gangrene agent. It will make him sick, but he will survive. He will not even scar too much. I detected the gangrene from the start.

The other head continued, but in a sneering voice.

–The pills are slow-release. He must take two a day. Night and morning. Put the salve on now and once a day when he wakes up in the mornings. He can take two of the yellow pills, immediately! That will give enough boost to start the healing process!–

Explain that he will be sick.

–For a couple of days!–

"All right!" Z snapped. The heads grew silent. Z turned

to the rider and explained he must take two of the pills now, then morning and evening, and use the salve daily. He explained he would be sick for two or three days.

"He will die," the head rider argued. "No one ever lives after he gets the creeping death. His blood will turn green and he will die. We have all accepted that. It is the way."

Z stared the rider down. "If he uses these things as I said and he dies, you may have the jar of the salve. It's pure gold. If he lives, the jar is his.

"If you think you'll kill him to get the jar, I'll do this little extra thing." Z circled the jar top three times with his hand, palm down and said, "Beelzebub!

"The jar is protected. If you harm this man, you'll be turned into a rock slug. The demon will come back to me when this man is dead or well. The jar will turn to stone, should I die."

Z turned back to the sick rider, showed him how to cover the sore with the salve, and had him swallow two of the pills. The group then turned from the riders and went toward town. The head rider came after them and said, "I would have a word."

–Here we go! Now you have to listen to every little ache and pain any of these toads have. Dunce!–

Now, No! You don't know that! Don't jump to those silly conclusions. Be nice!

"You two shut up. And No, you'd best remember who you're calling names," Z said, then turned to the rider. "What can I do for you?"

"Is that your castle?" the rider asked.

"Well, yes," Tom replied. "We sort of threw a little thing together for when we're in this area."

"Is it real gold?" the rider asked.

[It's only gold covered. Why? Too pretentious?]

"We're soldiers," the rider said. "We depend on good

hard bronze to protect us and gold to barter. Sorcerers always fall to hard bronze!

"I will give this advice. You have aided my friend and clanmate, therefore, you have aided me.

"I'm called barbarian, and I'm called mercenary.

"I was told that, should my band capture yon golden castle, we could have half the gold there. It was said there would be more than enough to buy my band any luxuries we could dream of for life.

"You have enemies. Best beware."

Z laughed. "Maybe, please make some gold for our friends here.

"The castle is protected by spells and demons beyond your imagination, but I thank you for the information."

He drew the widebladed knife from his scabbard and the rider placed a hand on the hilt of his sword.

"Yes, draw the sword," Z suggested. "I wish to show you something. It's a thing you and the others would do well to learn.

"This knife is made of what we wizards call chrome alloy vanadium steel. It's harder than any bronze, or even iron and will never tarnish or rust.

"Hold the sword out."

The rider held the sword out and Z made a hard slash at it. He meant to cut a notch in the sword, but the sharp knife sliced through the blade, leaving the rider holding a third of a meter of sword.

"This will kill a sorcerer, or even a wizard," Z promised. "Bronze will kill some sorcerers, but it'll be laughed at by a wizard."

He turned the shiny knife around and held the blade. He offered the handle to the rider. "This is yours," he said. "You're wiser than those who would attack us. I call you friend. Be wise enough not to depend on this knife against wizards and sorcerers. While it's proof against their magic spells, you aren't proof against a blade, even of bronze, in *their* hands.

"Tell your men the castle's only coated with very thin gold, though it contains unbelievable treasures. A wizard's treasures turn to dust when the wizard dies. It's foolish to covet them, unless you're a wizard, yourself. If you're even a halfway decent wizard, you can make your own fine treasures, so don't bother being greedy for such unimportant things. Should Tee try to trick you again, show him the knife and point out to him that you're well-protected. He's nothing more nor less than an ordinary man against that blade."

The rider grinned, which showed very bad teeth. "I didn't say it was Tee."

Tom grinned back and said, "But you didn't say it wasn't Tee, either."

"I guess I didn't, did I?" The rider grinned again.

Z took a solid lump of about ten kilograms of gold from the floater and handed it to the rider. "Divide this among your men. It'll make it worth their while to have come here. The people in that castle would have found a way to cheat you of anything you might have found, had you been able to invade our castle."

"If Varn is to be well it was worth a hundred trips," the rider replied. "I gave you his name, but I feel he's safe. You could've taken his soul if you wanted when you gave him the poultice."

He saluted with his new knife and rode back to his men, who turned and rode away with him, without a backward glance at the castle.

[Was it necessary to give so much, Z?]

"I did that to anger Tee," Z replied. "It'll be apparent to him we can buy more than he can. Anything I can do to make him lose his temper, I will. The knife'll scare hell out of him. Tom will tell you a sorcerer can turn bronze or any other non-ferrous metal to powder with one of the spells that really do work. It won't affect ferrous metals, and the knife was a stainless steel that's mostly iron. If we can get Tee mad and scared at the same time, he'll try something."

I don't mind baiting such as Tee. Each time I hear about this magic stuff, I get more worried. I don't want to anger the thing we came here about.

Tom laughed and replied, "That would really put us in the middle of swords and sorcery! We'd have a small chance, if any, of living long lives. It would be an interesting short life, though."

[I take it we will take our repast at Net's? It might be a good idea to make a few friends. My empathy tells me he's really a decent sort.]

"Take our repast?" Tom said. "Cripes! Are you going high class on us?"

[Humph! I have always been high class. You just haven't breeding and education enough to notice.]

They were entering Net's. Z waved for Net to bring wine.

"Not to notice class?" Tom returned. "You wouldn't know what class was if it came with a sign!"

–A classy rubber ball! Now I've heard it all!–

[Rubber is far more useful than bronze, and definitely more pleasant to be around.]

"Yeah," Tom said. "If you throw a rubber ball, it'll bounce. If you throw a bronze head you'll probably get a hernia."

–If you heat a rubber ball and throw it it'll go 'splut!' and stick.–

You shouldn't have said that!

–Why not, Copperpuss? Who asked you, anyhow?–

[This is why not!]

Thing made a couple of passes over No with a tentacle and it glowed red hot.

–Eeeeeeeeeee ooooooooo wah wah!–

You just won't learn! Don't say heat or cold around Maybe. Now your finish will discolor. If you would just try to be nice, for an enormous change, you wouldn't always be getting in these kinds of situations.

"You two stop it!" Z said.

Net came up with the wine and a plate of sweetcakes. Thing chilled the wine and said, [Any poison today?]

Z held the pewter plate of sweetcakes over the No head until it got too warm to hold.

"You have some use after all, Maybe," he said, and offered some of the cakes to Tom.

"You guys should get jobs at the castle. The jester there is really bad, not that *they'd* notice," Net said.

"Are you saying we're a bunch of clowns?" Tom asked.

Net looked nervous.

"Well, aren't we?" Z asked.

Net grinned and answered, "A lot better than that jester, anyway. I don't think you're like most of these sorcerers around here. They're all so, I don't know. Something. Nasty. They never smile, much less laugh. They don't make jokes. They don't have any fun, and they don't live life."

[That's the whole trouble. They don't live life.]

Net added, "I don't think there's any mean in you guys. You knew I'd poisoned the sweetcakes, but you knew it wasn't me, at the same time. Anyone else would have turned me into something nasty or made me eat the rest of them. You just thought it was funny.

"I don't know what that poison was, but the cakes that were left I put out back and it killed a big colony of alley rodents right out! Some good came from them, despite what, uh, the person who gave it to me planned!"

Tom grinned, and said, "Get Tee to make you and the rest of the merchants a bunch of it and you can get rid of the rodents around here. Life'll be easier. They won't eat all your expensive grain products.

"They carry the fever sicknesses, too. I don't care what the sorcerers say, there's always a lot of sickness when those things are too many in numbers. I've seen that everywhere I've been – and I've been a lot of places."

"Hey! That's an idea!" Net exclaimed. "Sorcerers are always looking for a way to make money, so we could buy the stuff from him."

[See how great life can be if you but think about the good things to do with all the things around you?]

–Now we get silly platitudes from the greatest minds of our times.–

Don't!

[Oh? Have you let the heat get to your head?]

Thing passed a tentacle over the No head and it was frozen into a block of condensing vapor.

[Is the wine getting warm, Boss?]

Really, Maybe, you'll ruin what little ability No has to think.

"Stop it," Z said.

Net giggled and walked away. He came back after a few more minutes with a large pan of a spicy-smelling stew.

"On the house," he announced. "You guys've already paid me enough to have a well put in the back. They're digging it now. In a few days I'll have chilled wine and my own fresh water!

"The water from the castle is good, though."

They tried the spicy stew (Maita said it was safe for Thing) and found it to be delicious. They ate, and Z left one of the gold coins on the table when they left.

"They definitely have garlic here," Z said. "Remember the amaranth? I said it was the same as on Earth?

"Well, they have garlic. It'll be the same as on Earth. It'll be little globs of whitish bulbs that you break off and grind up or squeeze the juice out of. *That* was real *garlic*!"

They were near the castle, where there were a variety of stalls set against the wall with vendors hawking various wares and produces. Thing went to a produce stall to ask if they carried the pungent spice they had eaten in the stew at lunch.

The woman showed several spices, but didn't know which they wanted. Tom went to her and said, "This one," and blew his breath in her face.

"Phew!" she cried. "You ate at Net's!" She took a handful of nuts from a pan on the shelf.

"Those look like pecans!" Z cried. He picked one up and cracked it. The smell of garlic was overpowering. He gave her a gold coin and took the whole pan. The old woman was staring open-mouthed at the fortune in her hand as they walked away.

"I'm going to show you how to make pizza and spaghetti and those great Italian dishes, Maita!" Z said. "Analyze this stuff. This is great! I have those mushrooms in the cave and that Micktian string cheese – lasagna, here we come!"

I can smell it over here, and I don't have any sense of smell.

They strolled around for almost an hour until they came upon a group of children and adolescents around an older man in a small tree-shaded square. They stopped to listen as he told the children stories and showed them how to write some words.

[A teacher.]

–Figured that out all by yourself, did you?–

Now, No. I warned you over and over....

"Shut up!" Z snapped quietly.

After awhile, the old man looked up and saw them. A silence fell and the children drew together.

Z went to the old man and urged, "No, don't stop. A teacher is the most important person in a community. What the community becomes over the years is what the teachers have taught them to be. Education can never be enough. Whatever you think you know, or whatever you learn, there is always more."

"A sorcerer who wants the children to learn?" the teacher asked. "How unique!"

Z said, "Ah! But the children must learn of life! Why else should a person, himself, learn, if not to pass his knowledge on? Of what use are your numbers if only one knows them? Can a word have use if only one knows it? Can that one communicate?

"There are few things of more importance than knowledge, thus few are people more important than those who can save that knowledge for the coming generations. Without teachers, all things would have to be repeated by all people. There could be no progress, no advancement."

"You have intelligence, I see," the teacher replied. "How, then, can you waste your time in the sorceries?"

"There's truth in all things, and there are falsehoods in all things," Z said. "Consider the grains of the fields.

"There is flour in those grains.

"That's like truth.

"To look at a grain kernel, one can't see the flour. One must study the kernel and dry it, then grind it. Only after one has dried the grain and ground it can he have the wonderful thing we call flour. Only after it is flour can it be used in so many ways.

"Only after you've inspected and worked with a thing can

you know its truth.

"One time, many thousands of years ago, one man learned this about the grain – that it could be ground into flour. If that man hadn't passed this truth along, would you have the flour today?

"You'll say that someone else would have discovered the secret of the grain, its truth. That is true, but someone had to pass it to another at some time, and that one had to pass it along, and so forth. Without the teachers, we would have no sweetcakes nor any bread nor much of the foods we eat.

"The sorcerer is necessary. He's the man who discovered the grinding of the grain the teacher taught others. It's a very sad thing today's sorcerers want all to be secrets. This is a thing that could cause great loss to all future people.

"There's no reason to find knowledge, if it is to become a dark secret. That is effort wasted. Once time is spent, the coin can't ever be returned. To learn a thing, only to keep that knowledge from others, is merely time forever lost to a losing cause – time better spent in other ways."

"You surprise me," the teacher said. "Why do you not want secrets?"

"I want some secrets," Z replied. "If I find a thing in my studies that will benefit my fellow beings, I've got the moral responsibility to pass it to a teacher, who can pass it on to others.

"I'll show you what I mean."

He took a globe of clear quartz that was hanging on a chain on his robe and held it up for the students to see.

"This is a piece of clear quartz. Nothing more," he stated. "All of you know there's a lot of it in the mountains. Most of you have some of it in your homes. It's pretty and does have some uses.

"I'll show you some of the things you can do with a piece

of polished quartz.

"This is a globe. I'll break it into a small piece of the globe."

He took Tom's knife to break a chip off.

"Notice that one side of the piece is rounded, while the other is flatter. I'll grind it totally flat."

He rubbed it on Thing's floater and had Maita shave and polish the bit out of sight.

"What I meant about secrets is that I'll show you what I can do, but you must discover how to do it. I use sorcery, but you can do almost anything sorcery can do, if you learn.

Now I have a piece of clear quartz that's flat on one side and round on the other. I'll hold it to the sun and the light will come to a point where the center of the globe was. That point, we'll call the focus.

"The first thing you must learn is that the focus is where the center of the globe was. Always.

"I will keep some secrets about what I know of quartz so you will seek for yourselves. I will tell you only enough to make you want to ask questions.

"Give me a piece of cloth or paper. Thank you.

"I'll put this piece of cloth on the ground and I'll put the piece of quartz so that the focus is a point of light on the piece of cloth.

"It's smoking ... it's burning.

"The reason is simple.

"You've all felt the heat from the sun for your entire lives. What this has done is take all the heat that's hitting the whole piece of quartz and has put it at the focus.

"Light is at the focus.

"We've now learned one fact, namely that all the light striking the piece is put at the focus. We've also learned we have some evidence indicating heat is a kind of light.

Other tests prove that, but you must never say a thing is true without being able to prove the thing and show it's true by different methods, unless it's enough to be self-evident.

"This should bring to mind a test.

"If the light is brought to a point at the focus from one direction, then the light at the focus should be spread away across the whole piece from the other, so we'll put the piece of cloth close to the focus point and look into the piece of quartz. If our theory is true, we'll see what's at the small focus across the whole piece and it'll look much larger.

"Everyone look. It works!

"Now you have a project for each of you to work on for years. You can call this shape a lens, which is what we wizards call a shaped piece of quartz, such as this, and you can make different lenses to see what shapes you can use to see more.

"What happens if the lens is backward? If it curves inward instead of outward? Can you put several lenses in a row and make a very small thing appear very big?

"We've only got one more thing to show that I've found about a lens.

"I hold it up and out and look through it – and everything is upside down and backward! See?

"So I must say that the light is coming out from the other side from where it came in. You must discover why.

"There may be thousands of things to discover about the lens. It's up to you to discover them. You may also discover much about light, at the same time."

"And about numbers!" the teacher cried. "You said the focus is at the center of the globe! That will mean it is a ratio of numbers! It may be possible to learn all about these lenses from numbers, and not have to make so many things."

"You may make theories with numbers, no more," Tom warned. "You'll have to make the theory, then make the lens to test it. If you rely too much on numbers, your mistakes will also be in an increasing ratio when the numbers are wrong."

"A wise demon!" the teacher said.

[We demons are only other people from other places with other ways. Only the golems are all magic. You can see how inferior that can make a thing.]

–Huh! Golems don't bleed. That's enough to make us superior.–

*That is not true! You don't bleed, but you are not *that* superior. You can't keep your mouth shut long enough to stay out of trouble. If there's anything you should have learned from Boss's little lecture, it's that you never learn! Not anything!*

–Shove it in your ear, Grain Brain! I didn't ask you!–

That's exactly what I mean! Why must you always be such a pain? Be nice.

–I'll nice your....–

"Quiet!" Z shouted. The children were giggling.

"That's the trouble with magic," Z sighed. "You can never really know what you're going to get. Some of it might be as bad as these golems!"

"But I am teaching the children that magic is only clever theater and trickery!" the teacher cried.

[No. It is mostly trickery, the way these so-called magicians around here use it, but not all.]

Z reached out and Thing moved onto his shoulder. The children gasped.

"The reality of magic isn't in some of the wild things we can do," he said, pointing at the little piece of cloth, which suddenly burst into flame. "If it were all only trickery, these demons would be people in costumes, or simply tricks of another sort. Come touch them, test them. They aren't tricks."

Tom went to the children, who backed away, except for one small child, who was awestruck. Tom picked it up and put it on his shoulder. It giggled, then some of the others came to touch him. Soon, they were all touching him and were even touching Thing's tentacles. The teacher was arguing with the No head, which was being insulting, while the Yes head was trying to be nice.

They stayed almost an hour longer, then went back to the fountain. There were soldiers there, and two very large and powerfully-built mercenaries. The two mercenaries wasted no time in coming up with drawn swords and threatening the group. Z grinned at Tom and they stood back-to-back and waited. They drew their swords and faced the barbarians.

The two mercenaries nodded at one another and charged.

It was a short thing. Z and Tom had steel swords sharpened to an amazing edge and inset with diamond for hardness. They used the fencing techniques from the crystals and were soon able to cut the blades off the bar-barian's swords. The barbarians then charged – and found themselves woozily semiconscious on the ground, a result of the karate of the crystals.

Z waved for the carpet to come down and looked around at the soldiers while it unfolded. He recognized the soldier from the clam incident who had said he wanted no part of magic. He grinned and got a grin in return. The group went back to their castle.

Well? Did we accomplish anything?

[We have instilled a sense of curiosity into a group of children. That was a truly great accomplishment. I'm sure this Martin will approve of that!]

Tom said, "We've acted unlike any sorcerers they've ever seen. We've shown deep compassion and caring for some barbarian mercenary. We've shown a sense of humor — even made jokes with a pub worker. We've taught a teacher. We've encouraged children to learn.

"We've accomplished one hell of a lot!"

"Now we wait awhile to see if Martin takes note," Z suggested.

The Castle

They waited two days and heard nothing.

"I would've thought that Martin would've had to come before this!" Z complained. "I don't understand it! We've surely made enough of an impression for him to be curious by now!"

"I said he wouldn't come," Tom said. "Why should he?"

[How could he?]

"What do you mean?" Tom asked.

[We are a bit off the main road, you know.]

Martin would have no trouble getting here, at all. I think he wouldn't have any trouble getting anywhere, if he's been to all of the worlds we suspect.

[Or he could send a messenger?]

"That would be no trouble," Z agreed.

[I'll say what I feel, then. We have gone to town twice now for the purpose of going to that castle. We haven't even walked into the open courtyard. Why not? Is there something to be so afraid of there – or is it just that you are afraid you will actually meet Martin at the castle?]

Z looked at Tom, who shrugged.

Because they want Martin to come to them. If they go to him, they lose the advantage. Right?

Tom grinned and said, "We're actually scared to brace the lion in his den, as Z would say. Thing's right about that."

"That's accurate. It's just what I'd say," Z said.

I know we agreed to let you run things, but you said you wanted us in it. Let's go to the castle. Now.

[I agree.]

"Okay," Tom said.

Z nodded. They went out to the flying carpet and thence

Page 91

(Thence?) to the fountain outside the castle gates, where they sent the floater up to wait for them. They strolled into the courtyard, then went to the big doors, where they were stopped by a palace guard, who was obviously nervous.

Z requested, "Just announce that Boss and his associates are here and would like to call on their new neighbors. We've recently moved to the near area and wish to know those of consequence around here. We'll leave it to your discretion as to exactly who is of any consequence."

The guard sent a page into the castle. The boy returned in a few minutes to ask the group to follow him. They were led into an enormous hall and through to a large room where a man and woman were seated on thrones. The page bowed low to the floor and backed away. A guard stepped forward and stuck a sword point in Z's face. "Bow," he ordered.

Z touched the sword end with the stun wand and the guard was thrown across the floor, where he ended laying against a column five or six meters distant.

Z smiled at the two on the thrones. He said, "We do not bow to mortals, and you sure look like mortals to me! There has two be two of you, Lady! No one woman could be *that* ugly!"

Another guard drew a bow, but the string broke when Tom pointed at it. (Maita cut it with a heat laser from the golem's floater.) Two more guards ran into the room and slid past the group and up against the steps that went to the thrones. (Maita made the surface of the floor vibrate with sonics until it was very slippery.)

Tom stepped forward and said, "This is going too far! I'm called Extrx and that's Yes and No and Maybe. He's Boss. We're merely calling to introduce ourselves to our new neighbors. I must say, this is hardly a cordial welcome! No wonder everyone we've talked to says you're a couple of snobbish pains in the ass!"

The woman said, "You would be wise to go as far from here as possible and as soon as possible. We don't fear demons in this court! Our wizard, Tee, will make short dispatch of the lot of you!"

[You lack the finer points of class. We are here and we have built a small chateau on the hill above you. We don't pick up and leave just because you are unfriendly! As far as Tee goes, we have met. Whoopee! I'm, as Boss quotes a person from his history, underwhelmed.]

–Give some people a little castle and they start thinking they're privileged over other people. You got that right, Maybe. No class. Boss sure pegged that ugly broad right! There should be three to be *that* ugly!–

Please try to control yourself. This is not your affair – even if I am finally forced to agree with you.

–Blow it out your ear, Air Brain. Nobody asked you.–

Why do you insist on embarrassing me wherever we go? Why am I given this burden to bear? Be nice. Why must you lower yourself to the level of these?

–I couldn't lower myself to their level with a crane!–

"Stop it!" Z said. "I'm afraid they're somewhat difficult at times, particularly around arrogant snobs, but I suppose you're used to that."

The man stood. "You have the insufferable effrontery to come here and act in this manner?!" he screamed. "I'll have you beheaded in the public square!"

Tom smiled sweetly. "We're merely reacting to the way we're being treated," he said. "If you're reasonable and kind to us, we'll treat you the same. If you insist on being a couple of asses, we'll treat you like asses."

"Guards! Guards!" the woman screamed. "A demon? A demon has the audacity to address us? In that manner? I will not have it! Guards! Seize them!"

–Oh, sit your silly fat ass down, Toad Puss. You become overly repetitions. Your voice is as ugly as your face!–

Now don't call that ugly broad Toad Puss, No. She looks more like a rock slug. You always do that. Doesn't accuracy mean anything to you?

–I hate like the hells to say anything, but I have to admit you're probably right, Globe Head. The old geezer looks worse than any of the demons I know – and I know a lot of demons.–

"You two knock it off," Z snapped, then to the count and countess, "They really are hard to control."

[But accurate. She does look more like a rock slug than a toad. Her beak is as sharp as a.... Remember those fish we saw down at Port Seascape? The ones that hid under rocks and uglied their prey to death? She looks like she should be a fish under a rock. She'd probably scare the rock.]

"I'd say *he* looks more like that fish you painted the oil study of by the islands, Maybe," Tom said. "You remember. The one you said looked like something from a failed pond ooze experiment that had spoiled, on top of it?"

The two sat again on the thrones. They were staring aghast at the group. The guards were carefully keeping their distance. A troop of soldiers came running into the room – and immediately fell into a heap of snoring men on the floor. Maita had used Thing's floater to sedate them.

"What did you do?" Z whispered to the floater.

Sprayed a bit of the instant sedative.

The woman was jumping up and down. "Get up! Wake up!" she was screaming.

–Doesn't she sound like that sliding door that sticks on the patio? The one Boss always cusses at?–

*You are saying more true things today! I am proud of

you.*

–Shove it in your stupid ... I guess you don't have one. I don't need your goody-goody words, Grease Face.–

"Stop it," Z said. "We will be going now. I can't say how long it's been since we were treated in the manner that you've treated us today. I doubt we've ever been so rudely received anywhere, but I suppose, if you were raised with the barnyard animals, you'll act like barnyard animals.

"I meant to invite you to our little place, but don't feel you would be too welcome, so must refrain. You lack the higher refinement of the Verfral tribesmen, so I suppose we'll invite them, instead.

"Come on guys."

They turned and were going out the door, still hearing the woman screaming they had the effrontery to turn their backs on her. They would pay dearly for the insult.

They then went to Net's to have lunch. Before they were through, Net came to them to say orders had been given that no one was to give them any service. "The order is directly from Countess Toot. She sent the army around to tell everyone."

"Toot?" Z said and broke out laughing.

"Substi-Toot for the prosti-Toot?" Tom said. He started laughing, too.

Tom was referring to a joke Z had told him.

"Are you asking us to leave?" Z asked.

"Not at all!" Net cried. "I just want you to know there may be soldiers looking for you. Be careful.

"I'd like to see them tell me who I can serve! That'll be the day when Hot Springs are frozen over!"

[We will handle any odd soldiers they send without doing damage to your establishment. I think you would have greatly enjoyed our little audience with the lovely countess and her handsome husband. We tried to figure just which fish each looked like, but they seemed to take offense! Strange people! No class at all!]

Net grinned and went back to the kitchen. A few minutes later, four soldiers came into the door and stopped. The lead officer was the one who had been at the clam. He grinned and said, "No one here." He saluted as the soldiers left.

Net came over and said, "Not many of the soldiers like the Count and Countess. You seem to have a friend in Ward."

"Is Ward the soldier?" Tom asked.

"Yes," Net replied. "He's my wife's brother."

They finished the snack and wine, then went back to the fountain, where Tee was waiting with twenty or more soldiers. Maita said, *Watch this.*

The floater moved slowly toward the castle. The soldiers followed. When it had led them all inside, it suddenly went up to laser the chain holding the bronze drop-gate. The soldiers watched through the grille as the group climbed onto the carpet and flew away. They went to their castle, where they sat around in the comfortable private room that was hidden from the rest of the castle. It was designed with more functional furniture, so far as Tom and Thing were concerned.

"I don't know what else we can do to draw Martin out," Z complained. "We've tried about everything I can think of! I'm now running out of ideas."

"I think he's enjoying this," Tom replied. "He's probably laughing his ass off about our little confrontation with the lovely Countess Toot."

They talked for awhile, until Maita said there was a band of mercenaries outside the rear gates. They seemed to have some kind of problem, but were also a bit afraid to approach this new kind of wizard and a bunch of assorted demons and golems.

"How did they get here?" Z asked.

Tom laughed. "There's a fairly good trail from the mountains," he said. "I found it when I flew over it the other morning."

[What do you want to do about them? Let them in?]

Z stood up. "I'll go see what they want," he said. "Maybe they're friends of the ones we saw at the castle. Could be they need a doctor for someone."

Z went out and to the rear gates, where he found thirty or so of the barbarian mercenaries. "Good afternoon," he said. "What can I do for you?"

"We respectfully request an audience with the one called Boss," the lead rider said.

"I'm Boss," Z answered. "What can I do for you?"

"But you're a demon!" one of the riders cried. "You act as your own page?"

Z laughed. He said, "We're sort of informal around here. I'm not a demon, I'm a wizard – well, perhaps a little of both.

"You may leave your mounts in the rear court here. Just close the gates so they won't wander off. There's good water for them."

The two-headed floater appeared and came over his head.

"Yes and No, please see that all the animals are fed," Z requested.

–I ain't cooking for this bunch. It ain't my job. What the hell you got Harpiscrud in there for?–

He didn't ask you to cook. Just see that the mounts are fed.

–Up yours, Lead Head! Nobody asked you. You always stick your stupid ugly nose where it ain't wanted!–

"Stop it," Z demanded. "I didn't ask you to feed the

mounts, I told you to. Get at it, *now*! – or I'll send Maybe out here to supervise!

"Come on in," he continued. "That's Yes and No – I'm sure you can figure which is which."

The head rider said, "I'm Vorn. May I leave a guard here with the mounts?"

"It isn't necessary," Z said. "They'll be well taken care of. You have my word."

They went into the large dining hall, where the table was covered with exotic foods and wines. Thing was on the floater over the center of the table.

[Please be seated! Eat, drink! We only ask that you do not overindulge in the wines. A drunk is most unpleasant company – unless it's oneself.]

They all looked nervous and even more so as Tom came into the room.

"Please," Vorn said. "We come to ask aid. We will cause you no trouble. We won't fight your demons."

Tom laughed. "Don't worry about me!" he called. "I want to get a little snack. We don't go around fighting all the time. We'd rather enjoy life. Let those stupid sorcerers at the castles fight each other. Leave us out of it.

"How do you need our aid?" He picked up some fruit and dropped into a chair.

Z waved at the table and said, "Sit! Eat! The demon over the table is called Maybe and that is Extrx.

"What can we do for you?"

A couple of the riders tasted some of the food and looked surprised. They sat to begin eating. Soon all of them were at the table.

"We have heard of your help to Varn, who would be dead by now, but who is over even the fever, today," Vorn said. "We have some treasures and we'll work for you, if you will aid us."

"We ask no silly treasures," Z replied. "Look around. What possible treasure would we want? I can make anything we want or need – or the demons will make it for us. The goblet in your hand has more jewels than the tiara that Countess Poop wears."

"She is called Countess Toot," Vorn corrected.

The two-headed floater had come in. It was behind and above Z.

–I prefer Poop. It sounds like that ugly slug looks. Like a particularly smelly fart.–

Don't interrupt people when they are talking. Show some manners. You weren't raised that way!

–Put it in your ear and blow it out your nose, Beak Face. I thought I was going to have to cook all this for these animals. As far as the way I was raised, I was cast, and you know it.–

You should learn when to keep your mouth shut.

–Why, Puke Puss?–

[Because of this! You like to cook?]

–Oh, no!–

Thing passed a tentacle over No and it was glowing red hot again.

–Eeeeeeeeee ooooooooo hee!–

You simply won't learn! I try and try, but you just refuse to listen! Now your shine is all gone and you'll have to bribe a minor demon to polish you again – heee! – and again – and again! Heee!

"You two stop it!" Z ordered. The barbarians were enjoying the show immensely.

Vorn said, "Please! We need your help. Tell us how we can pay you."

"We don't charge for our help," Tom answered. "Either we decide to help or we decide not to. Tell us what your problem is."

"Some sorcerer put an evil spell on all of our people in the forest," Vorn said. "Many are dying. We need help. We can't find out how to stop it. We don't know why it was done!"

"How are they dying?" Z asked.

"They get the witch fever!" Vorn cried. "They can't eat and the fever burns up their minds! We can't stop it!"

[We should go to where the sickness is. We can work much better that way.]

"It's two days ride into the forest," Vorn said.

Boss can take the carpet and Maybe. You can be there in a few minutes. Vorn will go with you to show you the way.

"Me?" Vorn squeaked.

"Yes," Z replied. "Your men can remain here as our guests until we return. Come with me." He switched to Maitan to say, "Maita, be careful. You sounded like No making a reasonable request."

Vorn was extremely nervous, but came with Z to the tower, where they climbed onto the carpet and flew from the rampart. They flew for a few moments longer before Vorn's curiosity overcame his fear. He began to delight in the sensation until Z had to warn him not to go too close to the edge.

They arrived at an encampment, where everyone was hiding until Vorn stepped off the carpet and called. Z was then shown several of the people who were feverish, and the body of one who had recently died. Maita used the facilities hidden on the floater to check them over and said it was a bacteriological infection. Maita produced large quantities of oxytetracycline in slow-release pills and the barbarians were told to all take two a day for ten days and not to take more nor less.

Z burned some incense and tried to look as magician-like

as he could until the source of the contamination was found. Maita had the floater and Thing search the close area. They found a badly contaminated stream nearby. When the floater returned, Maita told Z a large animal carcass a bit upstream was the source. It was removed. Z warned everyone to stay away from that stream for ten days and nights to give his counter spell time to work. He said the spell came from the water and that, should this kind of sickness ever start again, the people were to stay away from where they were getting the water at the time.

"The spell is usually for only a hundred days, which is a long time to carry water from another place, but it's worth it if no one else gets sick and dies!" he said as they got back on the carpet to leave.

They went back to the castle to give the riders there the pills and told them how to take them.

"Where's Extrx?" Z asked when he failed to find him at the castle.

"He went out of the room a short while ago and didn't come back," one of the riders said.

Vorn tried to insist on some way of repaying the group, but Z assured him no payment was needed. Soon the sated happy barbarians rode off. Z stood and waved at them until they were out of the gate, then raced back into the castle.

"Maita! Where is Tom?" he shouted.

How would I know?

"The golems are here. The ship's here," Z said. "Where is he? We have to find him!"

[Maita, Z is very afraid. So am I.]

He's on the upper eastern tower, speaking with a demon, a Frome.

"From the castle?" Z asked.

*I assume so. I've kept the golems here by his request.

The demon is another type of large bird-like beings from another plane. It's much like the ones I took home. There will be few Mesorchii here, but a number of Fromes are on the planet.*

Z and Thing went up to the high tower, where they found Tom and the large bird-like person who had been seen there when the castle was still under construction.

"Yo, Z," Tom greeted him. "We have something of a problem, I think. This being wants me to arrange for it to go home, but I don't know if Maita can take it if it doesn't know which plane it's from. It seems the fact it came here means it can't return to the sorcerer who brought it to Tlorg. That would be suicide."

"Martin?" Z asked.

"Marteen do not breeng to here," the bird said. "Marteen forbid breeng to here Frome."

"Who does?" Z asked.

"Tee," the bird answered.

Z went to the door of the tower and called out, "Maita!" Thing came up on the floater.

What?

"Can you find how to get our friend here home?" Z asked.

[Is it escaping from Martin?]

"No. Tee," Z said. "It says Martin doesn't bring demons here and forbids others to bring them."

I can take it home if it will allow me to use the probe machine on it to find its natural plane. I knew from before how to return the Mesorchii, but I don't know the plane for Frome. It will have all the information in some part of its mind.

Tom asked, "If you can get it to its plane, can you find its planet?"

*Yes. Its planet will have a relative position quite close

to this one. Probably this same planet on another plane, or Tee couldn't bring it here. You are one of the Frome?*

"Zhess," the demon answered. "Called I be Goolik."

Tom explained it was necessary to use the machine, which would read all there was to know about it. The bird agreed.

Maita took the bird home, after making them all promise they wouldn't leave the castle until it returned. It was only gone a bit more than two hours.

"We're going to town," Z said when Maita was back. "The demon looked just like a Mesorchii. What's the difference?"

"Another planal mode. An easier one. I doubt anymore Mesorchii will be brought. Those were probably brought by accident. Go to town?*

[What do you have in mind?]

"I'm going to face one sorcerer down," Z said. "I've run across this Tee character one time too many. If Martin made some kind of decree that says the demons aren't to be called, we're going to enforce it for him, in this case!"

They all got aboard the carpet, after putting on clean costumes, and went to the square by the fountain. People now were a bit curious about them and would stare.

They sat around the fountain bench to wait. After a few moments the old woman they bought the garlic-like spice from came to them.

"Sirs," she said. "I would a word with you."

"Certainly," Tom replied. "What is it?"

"The Countess has taken the gold coin. She said it was sorcerers gold and was worthless. I know that's not true, but I'm a weak old woman who can't resist her soldiers," she explained. "You've done good deeds in defiance of her. Many say you're good. We all know she's not.

"We ask your help. We ask only that she don't bother us

no more. That's not much, perhaps, but it's more than we can do."

Z handed her two of the coins. "Take these," he said and raised his voice. "Any of my coins that are freely given or spent are good. Any that are taken will bring great grief to the taker. This I swear. The Countess Toot has caused the coin to be taken from this honest woman. You will see her reward."

The old woman bowed, thanked them, and left.

"Maita, can you give that vicious old broad some kind of spectacular, er, affliction?" Z asked. "Something that will be easy to see or that will at least be evident to anyone in her presence."

Yo! I'm sure I can think of something.

They stayed by the fountain. About half an hour later, a lot of activity started around the castle. People came and went while the soldiers were milling about.

"What did you do?" Tom asked the floater.

I did a little thing to her body chemistry while she was napping in her tower. It seems her ugly body has developed a rather unpleasant odor. Sort of like rotten eggs. She's very red-faced about it.

After a few minutes longer a page came to them. He was terrified of them, but more afraid of what was going on in the castle.

"You are ordered to go to the castle reception room," the page said to Z.

"Tell the Countess I said to stick her dirty feet in her mouth and see if she can manage to wiggle her toes," Z responded. "If you see the one they call Tee, tell him I can wait as long as necessary. He'll have to face me, sooner or later. You can see we're very comfortable here."

The page went back to the castle and a group of about a hundred soldiers marched out to surround them. Z raised

an eyebrow and Thing went above them and to one side
while the golem floater went up and to the other.

"You're not really going to try any of this stupidity are
you?" Z said. "Surely Tee has seen by now that he can't
keep hiding behind everybody else in the town! Tell him
to get his ass out here!"

"Sorcerer, you can't fight all of us," their captain said. "I
don't have any use for your type, as it is, so don't give me
any excuse to cut you up a little. I might enjoy something
like that more than you'd know!"

[With what?]

Thing waved a tentacle. A moment later the soldiers
were screaming and trying to get out of their clothes. They
dropped their weapons, which were quite hot.

Z said, "Micro waveth stoppeth.

"What were you saying, Captain? I couldn't hear well for
the noise."

"I despise your rotten stinking sorcerer's guts!" the
captain yelled. "You're nothing but cowards! You fear to
fight in an honest fight!"

Z said, "We aren't the cowards. We didn't bring a hundred troops with arms to capture a couple of demons and
a golem or two.

"I'll be most happy to enter into a contest with you, no
tricks, no magic. I'll kick you from one end of this square
to the other in unarmed combat, or prove I'm a better
swordsman than you. It's your choice to make, but don't
come here with all those troops and call the four of us
cowards or you'll eat your words – without salt."

"I'll name a champion!" the captain said.

[You *are* a coward, captain. I thought you were to lead
your troops. Why do you fear to fight Boss, personally? If
you so despise a coward, explain why you then wish to
have anyone substitute for you in single battle? Is it self-

hate you speak so in-elegantly of?]

"I fear no man!" the captain shouted. "I fear no demon!"

Oh? Then why would you want to select a champion, Muck Mouth? You never make any sense!

–Who cares? He's a coward and an ass. Boss can beat any champion this turd head can produce. For once, I'm glad you agree with me, Yes!–

*Don't be that way, No. Just because the captain is an asshole is no reason for you to be insulting to him. I merely called him Muck Mouth because he looks like he's been out grubbing for worms with his face. It was a comment on things as they are, not an insult. I rather doubt one *could* insult Muck Mouth.*

–Go stick your tongue against the stove and see if it's hot, Bubble Brain. Boss didn't ask for your advice.–

"You two stop it," Z said. "No has a bad habit of saying what we think of you. It has no tact. You can see that here, rarity of rarities, Yes even agrees – in this particular rare case."

"I don't know what you have hidden under all that cloth!" the captain said. "I can kill you in one minute or less in a fair fight. You don't have a chance in honest competition!"

Z grinned at him and Tom said, "You will both remove all your clothing. You will be allowed no weapons. Only your own heads, hands, and feet. No one will interfere on either side."

"Wait a minute!" Z cried in Maitan. "What's this about no clothing at all?"

[Why not? These people aren't overly inhibited, like you. You can't start making exceptions for your own psychological reasons. Take them off.]

Tom added, "I don't wear any clothes except this belt, anytime. There aren't any Earthmen or women here. Grow up a little!"

–Hey, Fur Face! I'm supposed to have the biting lines!–

[You don't have a copyright on them.]

Hey! Who asked you? Go float under a waterfall, Balloon Brain!

–Hey! Hey!–

I forgot.

"Okay," Z said. "Knock it off."

The captain was tearing his cloak off. "I'll show you what's funny!" he shouted.

Z sighed and removed the robes and folded them carefully. He dropped them on the bench by the fountain and turned just as the captain charged with a wild round-house swing. Z spun, caught the arm and twisted as he threw a hip under the big captain, who went sailing into the fountain.

"I wasn't ready!" Z cried. "No fair! Cheater! Cheater! No fair! You didn't say 'May I'!"

Some of the soldiers began to snigger.

The captain climbed onto the lip of the fountain. He dove at Z yelling, "Yaaaah!" Z stepped to the side and the captain went sprawling into the dirt.

"That was stupid!" Z chided. "Always be sure you have a nice soft place to land if you dive at something."

Hey! You got dirt in the muck!

A number of the soldiers were now having trouble controlling their laughter. The captain got to his feet and stood staring at Z. He looked like he would explode.

"Gee, captain," Z remarked sympathetically. "You seem to be bleeding. Must be the altitude. Do you often get nosebleeds? I can make a little remedy you can have for a mere five coppers!"

"Yaaah!" the captain screamed and came at him again. Z flipped him into the fountain again.

"I thought you only yelled that when you were nosediving into the ground," Z chided. "You really did need to rinse off, though. As Yes said, you were getting dirt in the muck."

The soldiers weren't trying to stop laughing anymore. Z saw Ward among the soldiers and winked at him. Ward saluted.

The captain was against the lip of the fountain again. Z held out a hand. "Let me help you out of there," he said.

The captain grabbed his arm, yelled, "Yaah!" and tried to yank. Z jumped and dove toward the captain, who was expecting resistance, so was thrown back against the fountain base, where his head bounced off a concrete projection. He was out cold. Z carried him to the fountain edge, where Tom lifted him out and laid him along the bench.

Z was on the lip of the fountain, climbing out, when Tom yelled, "Yah!" and dove at him, making a flying tackle and driving them back into the cool fountain pool. They put on a wild tumbling wrestling exhibition for a couple of minutes, then Z went to the edge of the pool.

"Come on in. The water's fine," he said to the soldiers.

Ward stepped out of his cloak and dove into the fountain. "You guys are total crazies!" he said. "Fane and Net said you were alright!"

Soon, six or eight of the soldiers were in the pool with them. When the captain regained consciousness, he stared at the scene for a moment and stomped into the castle gates.

"Hey!" Z called, "You forgot your clothes! Countess Poop will be mortified!"

Some of the soldiers followed him into the castle yard.

"We'd better get out and be ready," Tom suggested. "I'm afraid our good captain will be back with some kind of reinforcements.

"Didn't he seem angry to you guys? I wonder what got him all upset? Was it something I said?"

Ward laughed along with them. He signaled for the rest of the soldiers to get out of the fountain. They dressed, saluted and went into the castle yard.

[You are about to have company.]

They looked toward the castle gate to see red robes, flanked by four soldiers, coming toward them. Z slipped into his robes while Tom belted the sword and knives back around his waist.

"You are under arrest," Tee said.

"Kiss my ass," Z returned.

"These guards won't be affected by your petty spells," Tee said haughtily.

"Our petty spells have taken four of your demons away from you, routed your army and made you appear to be the fool you are," Tom pointed out. "We wanted to talk with you is the reason for this display out here, though I must admit – I enjoyed the swim."

The guards drew their swords. Z saw they were covered in glowing runes. He waved at Thing, who moved over the guards and waved a tentacle. The swords grew hot and the runes got brighter. Suddenly there was a "pop!" and the runes went out. The guards dropped the swords.

"If that's the best you can do, you'd better quit while you're ahead," Tom counseled. "Those little spells aren't going to do any good against Boss."

[He isn't ahead. He's way behind. Four demons, an army, an ugly old harridan who he has convinced he had some minor power, her husband, who looks like a fish, but doesn't have as much intelligence, and assorted devices are just the cost, to this point. I call that debit spending.]

–I call it stupid. How is the ugly old rock slug? I hear she has a stinking bad disposition, lately. She's supposed to be very red-faced about it.–

Must you start? Can't the others have a simple normal conversation without you making a spectacle of yourself?

–Why don't you use yourself in a test of the breaking point of bronze? You could stick that silly looking head in a vice and measure the pressure at which it splits.–

You could test which acids affect bronze fastest.... I forgot again.

"You two stop it," Z said. "How is Countess Poop?"

Tee drew himself up and looked down his nose at Z. "Her name is Toot!" he snapped.

"You remember," Tom said. "Toot. As in prosti-Toot."

"I warn you, pretenders!" Tee cried. "Watch your tongues while you still have them."

–What'll you do, Slug Brain? Put a *magic* spell on us? I'm so scared!–

No is right. Your spells don't seem to hold up well. Are you sure you read the right recipe? A rancid spell just isn't very ... acceptable in polite society.

–Can't you stay shut the hells up for ten crummy seconds, Bucket Mouth?–

"Stop it!" Z ordered.

"You will regret this!" Tee stormed. "Oh, yes. No one makes a fool out of me! No one!"

"I wouldn't think of trying to make a fool out of you," Z replied. "You're doing fine without our help."

–Where do you get this stuff? Henny Youngman?–

What do you know about Henny Youngman?

–I read it in Boss's mind. Next he'll be saying, 'Take my countess – please!'–

"Don't get started," Z said. "I want to say something to Tee here. I suggest he listens very carefully.

"If you call up one more demon, I'm going to send you to a sorcerer on the demon world. You'll be the demon there, where you'll be treated as you treat those you bring here.

"Think about it! You're a pitiful excuse for a sorcerer who is giving those who have some education and knowledge a bad name. Few are so sordid as you. You disgust all sorcerers worth the label. You seem to think, because you are able to fool a few locals, you can fool us. You think we'll believe you have power.

"The only one who believes that is yourself! You *are* a fool, so no one has to make one of you.

"Don't get before me again. Go crawl into whatever hole you crawled out of and remain there. Your childish delusions will eventually destroy you. That is inevitable!"

Tee drew himself up. "I am a friend of Martin," he said. "You anger me at your own risk. Be warned you had best leave this place before you anger Martin! He doesn't forgive such as you!"

[I have never seen a smile nor heard a small laugh from one of you sorcerers. You don't enjoy life. I can't believe Martin is at all like you. Martin has decreed no one call demons, yet you continue in defiance of his requests. You are a liar. You fear Martin. You are definitely *not* his friend!]

"Martin would never cavort around in some public fountain, unclothed, with a bunch of soldiers and demons," Tee snapped sharply. "Martin would not lower himself to grapple and fight with others. Martin shows proper decorum at all times. You feel that fun is so important? What has it ever done?"

"I can't explain color to one who has no sight," Z answered. "A symphony has no meaning to one who is deaf."

"I have sight!" Tee responded. "I hear!"

"No," Z countered. "You have eyes, but you can't see.

Worse, you won't see.

"You have ears that will not hear the truth.

"You stand before me and pose and preen like you're of importance to something, somewhere. You think you're powerful because you know a few simple spells. You are *not*! Your life is a waste of energy.

"You have ears, but will not hear, so I'm wasting my time speaking to you. Either you'll stand here and challenge me with your petty spells, or you'll go back into that castle and skulk behind the skirts of that ugly rock slug in there. I think you're too much of a coward to face me in contest. You face only those who you can hide from behind soldiers or some woman."

Tee fidgeted, then turned to stalk back toward the castle. The crowd that had gathered opened to let him stamp through among loud mutterings about cowards. He couldn't take it and spun, lifting his hands to point all the fingers at Z as he cried, "Azrathamantrum!"

Bolts of something very like electricity shot from the fingertips and Z put up a hand. Thing was pointing all four tentacles at Tee and Tom pointed the steel sword at him. The bolts seemed to bounce off of Z's hand and back to Tee, who screamed and burst into flames. In less than a minute, a heap of gray ashes lay where Tee had been.

Z shook his head and waved to the carpet, which came down and picked the group up. They went back to their castle and Tom carried Z to Maita, where they put him in a medical box. He had dropped unconscious as soon as he was on the carpet. It was several hours before the box opened and Z got out.

[What was it, Z? I was going to absorb some of it, but it didn't come near me. I thought it was electricity. It wasn't, at all. I didn't think such as Tee could control such vast power! I can't find what it was!]

*I couldn't do anything! I couldn't even analyze it! It should have killed you. I don't know why it didn't. That was a *very* powerful bolt. It was possibly something like the gestalt backwash that destroyed that planet out near EC (Book three: *Pirates*, and Book four: *Tristar*)!*

"I wasn't able to ground much of it with the steel," Tom said. "I was too far to the side. You have a lot more power than I thought. You should be dead. I wouldn't have gambled that you could turn that bolt."

Z replied, "I almost didn't. I thought I was a goner. Tee was a hell of a lot stronger than he was letting on. I think he was trying to trick Martin into giving him more power or into leaving so he could take over the area, personally. We may have stopped a very dangerous thing here. I think we might just meet Martin, now. I don't see how he can refuse to show up after this. I think we've shown him a lot of what Tee was planning."

[I sort of think Martin knows exactly what Tee was doing. Perhaps he will come now.]

Ward knew he was in for some mouth from the captain, but he didn't really very much care. The weird sorcerer and his even weirder demons were great fun. That made it worth listening to that storm-mouthed vacuum-head puff and blow a little.

He, Ward, had actually wrestled with a real demon in that pond! He didn't know demons could even go into water, and that one had the courage to actually tackle his sorcerer! They had thrown each other around in the most amazing way and had even invited trained soldiers to join them!

Net said they were different. He hadn't been joking. Sorcerers who had fun, who laughed and made jokes and who physically wrestled in a public fountain. It was wonderful! It was unheard of, but was something to remember. It was well worth one of old wind-mouth's rants.

Now it was going to splatter on the courtyard, though. Everyone had thought of that wizard and his demons as some kinds of jesters. Clowns, they called themselves. Just more loafers and wastrels.

Ward had seen Boss turn Tee's bolts, then had watched Tee burn to gray ashes there outside of the gates. The Count and Countess didn't have the intelligence to see that wizard had far more power than Tee ever hoped to hold. Boss must, therefore, truly be known to Martin, if he wasn't, in fact, a close friend and colleague of the great wizard.

Things could take a very nasty turn around here if they tried to challenge such awesome power! Tee plotted and schemed ways to fool Martin, which showed right there who was the fool. This one held that power already, yet Net said he didn't want to challenge Martin in any way.

Well, he didn't care! He had found people he could like in even a strange demon. He would *not* deny that liking!

The Countess was staying to her quarters. Her personal maids said she was a shocking sight – and that she smelled of the rotting waire eggs and the gorpnut spice that Net used in his stews. The spice tasted great, but the breath, for long hours afterward, would knock a roteater bird off of a dung wagon!

The wizard said she would pay dearly for her treatment of those who had done no harm to her or to them. Boss truly was, apparently, as good as his word!

Ward did worry about his brother-in-law, Net, though. Both Net and his sister were in danger from the Count and Countess. They had accepted gold from Boss.

The teacher said Boss couldn't really be a wizard, but was stuck as to the demons. No one could deny they were truly demons! Who but a wizard or sorcerer could control demons? Would a mere sorcerer dare call demons among his friends?

They were obviously close friends. No one was really in charge in that group. No sorcerer Ward ever heard of had any friends, much less demon friends. The demons hated them!

And the golems? Could anyone deny them? Even Boss was often driven to distraction by their constant bickering, but they were great fun, despite that – actually, because of that. They taught everyone around them all kinds of things in strange ways.

Boss had given wizard's secrets to the children. The child, Verona, had always been the smartest child in town. She had taken what Boss showed her much further than even such a great wizard could have guessed.

True wizard, clown, demon, wastrel, loafer – whatever he was, this town would never be the same! That, alone, meant he couldn't be all bad.

The group waited again for two days and nothing happened. They could see the town and couldn't but notice there were more soldiers around the castle than before – a great many more, and better armed.

The morning of the third day Z said, "I think I'd like to eat lunch at Net's today. I could use some of his stew."

I can make the stew exactly the same. If you want to visit the town, say so!

Tom replied, "The stew isn't important and neither is a visit to Net's. Martin's having fun at our expense. He's simply going to outwait us."

[I would like to go into town, too. It's fun.]

Whatever. I'm going to give Yes the tone Ape had and will put the golems on a separate unit that will program itself over a basic program. This tone will be Yes. (+)

They waited until nearly noon and took the carpet to town. Quite a few people stared almost hostilely at them as they put the tube in hover. Ward came running from the castle courtyard.

[Hello, Ward. How have you been?]

"Hello Maybe," Ward said. "Boss, they arrested Net!"

"Why?" Tom asked. "Net hasn't done anything at all!"

"For serving you and for having your coins," Ward reported. "The countess made either thing illegal. She had several of the vendors arrested."

"Come on," Z said, and marched toward the courtyard. When they came to the gate, two soldiers stepped in front of them. Z slapped them with the stun wand and kept right on going without missing a step.

The guards at the door dropped a metal gate, then turned in time to get slapped themselves by the wand. Maita lasered the gate and they went into the hallway, where they were quickly confronted by six more soldiers. Maita used the microwaves on their weapons, but one of them tried to grab Tom. Tom flipped him and rendered him unconscious with a chop.

The doors to the throne room were closed with bars across the inside. The laser cut through them like they were thin paper. There were two attendants with the count in the room.

Z walked to the count and said, "Where is Toad Face?"

The count demanded, "Get out of here! I will have you scum hung!"

Z turned the wand low and tapped the count, who was flung to the floor, where he lay gasping and retching. Z stood over him and said, "Where's that rock slug you're married to?"

The count whimpered and shook his head. Z slapped him with the wand again.

"I won't ask again!" he snapped. The count pointed to a door to the rear of the thrones. Z went to the door and kicked it in. There was a staircase going up behind the door. He went up the stairs and slammed into a tower room.

The countess was seated by a window. Z stopped short and stared. Her entire head was a bright crimson.

I told you I left her red-faced!

–It's an improvement, but then, anything would have to be.–

"Don't start!" Z snapped. "Well, countess. I see you've taken it on yourself to start arresting anyone who's cordial or even civil to us. That's hardly polite. I'm going to make you so sorry you were ever born, you're not going to believe it! You're going to beg me to let you die!

"I'll tell you now. Don't waste your breath. You're going

to have fame for as long as there are people on this world. Your name will live as an example of all that's disgusting in your race. Your very name will be used as a swear word for thousands of years.

"You will be known as Toot the Ugly. I'll see your name is reviled more than any other ever was or ever will be! You learn nothing, no matter the teacher or the method.

"We'll see! We'll just *see*!"

[Where are our friends being held?]

The countess stood with a hand at her throat. She didn't move. Tom took his knife from the calf sheath. He touched her throat with the tip. "You were asked a question," he purred. "When we ask you a question, you will answer it. You will answer quickly and honestly.

"I won't kill you. I'll just disfigure you a little. You are obviously a vain woman. Think of how you're going to look, soon, if you insist on being stupid."

"They are in the dungeons," she said. "You will shortly join them."

Tom shoved her and she went against a chair and ended on her knees on the floor.

–Watch your mouth, Red. You're on a short ration of our patience here.–

+Now, No!+

"Don't start – yet," Z said. "You golems can stay here and watch this sewage while I let our friends out of the castle dungeons."

He turned toward Toot. "Every indignity and hurt they've suffered will be returned to you tenfold. You have the word of Boss on that little item."

They went down the stairs and into the throne room. Only one attendant was in the room.

"Where are the dungeons?" Tom demanded.

"Under the castle. Where else?" the attendant sneered.

He got a kidney punch for his effort.

"I didn't hear you!" Tom said.

The attendant pointed to another massive door to the side. The group went through the door and down several flights of stairs, coming up against a heavy grille gate with a bronze door behind it. Maita cut the grille and the door completely off their brass hinges. They came on another thick bronze door with a small grilled opening in the center. Maita cut this door off its hinges, too.

There were two guards with rings of keys in a small office just inside the door. They put their hands on top of their heads and stood against the wall as soon as they saw the group coming.

"Open the cells and let all the prisoners out!" Z ordered.

The guards went down the narrow hall and opened all the doors. They went into some cells and released the chains on the prisoners.

From the first two cells came two women. One was the old woman who had sold them the spices.

"Were you mistreated here?" Z asked.

"Jist locked up," she said. "They took all my wares and my money."

[They will be returned to you tenfold.]

Net ran up and hugged the other woman. "Have you met my wife?" he asked. "This is Fane.

"This is Boss, who liked your famous stew so – and Extrx and Maybe."

Tom smiled at her. He said, "We were coming to have lunch at your place when Ward said you'd been arrested.

"Were any of you harmed?"

Net said, "No. They only locked us up and took our property. They would wait until the holiday to make examples of us."

[They are going to buy the whole block where your pub

is located and deed it permanently to your family. They are going to give you ten times the cash they took and ten times the supplies they destroyed. They are going to wish shortly they had never been born. They wish now they had never heard of Boss and his demons!]

The two guards had been slowly sidling toward the door. They suddenly broke and ran. Thing was suddenly ahead of them and daring them to come farther.

"They're going to do something stupid," Tom said. "We'll go up the stairs first. You people be ready to duck or run."

They started up the stairs and a ball of fire flew down at them. Thing dove from the floater and Tom caught it. The floater flipped up sideways and used the gravity grid in reverse to send the fireball back up the stairs. It was made of a large wad of cloth soaked in oil and resin and rolled down on them, after being ignited. There were some loud screams from above, then the floater sedately returned. It was quite a sight with the robes looking like a body with no head. It went right to Thing, who climbed back on.

They went up the stairs and stepped over the two bodies laying there, then went into the throne room and found it empty. Ward and another soldier came into the room, so Z told him to see the prisoners were home safely and that they were not again disturbed. They searched the castle from the dungeons upward and found the cash room behind the thrones on the other side from the tower door. They sent small chests of money to Net and to the old spice dealer. They found three of their coins there in a special little box, which Z put into a pocket in his robe.

They finished the search four and a half hours later and went back to the countess's tower room, where the golem heads were arguing steadily. When they entered the room, Z ordered, "Stop it, you two.

"Well Countess Toot the Ugly, how are you feeling?"

"I have listened to those two heads arguing for hours!" she cried. "I thought they would drive me crazy! It was most indecent of you to leave me at their mercy! I thought I would be driven insane!"

[Too late to save her! Let's go home, guys. The ugly toad isn't going anywhere, you can bet. We have a little thing or two we have to talk over.]

When they were walking back through the throne room, Ward was talking to the captain of the guards. The count was there. He tried to hide behind the captain.

"You have a new government, now," Z declared. "The count will act as call page and the captain is now latrine officer. Ward is the captain of the guard.

"Meet your new tyrant." He waved at the golem heads.

Ward grinned and said, "I await your orders. If you two are going to argue over everything, I'll have to select which I think will have given the best argument."

[That's all you can do. They don't agree on much.]

–Hey! He was talking to me, Balloon Face. When we want your worthless advice, we'll ask for it!–

+It is what will have to be. You will argue about every small thing.+

–I didn't ask you, Static Head! I just made a comment. Why don't you shut the hells up!?–

+If you would pause to consider what you are going to say, I'm sure you wouldn't say it!+

"You two stop it," Z said. "Let's go guys. We have to pass some ideas around."

They went to the fountain, where they climbed aboard the carpet amid cheers, then went to their golden castle and into the private room, where Maita had a servo bring them some stew identical to that served at Net's.

Okay. I've been patient above and beyond the call of duty. Where the hell is Martin and his laboratory?

[I'm wondering about that. We didn't see any evidence of it in the castle.]

"Oh, it was there," Tom said. "We just went all around it."

No, we didn't. I did measurements all over that castle. We didn't miss anything.

"Sure we did," Z said. "Maita, you're used to being up against those you're superior to in one area or another. This is a different situation."

Then you tell me how he could do it!

"What would your measurements show you about a room that was in another plane?" Z asked.

Another plane?

"Is there an echo in here?" Tom asked.

Do you think he could do that?

"It's a simple thing to bring demons from several other dimensional planes," Z said. "Why not put a room in one? Isn't that basically what our own power spheres are? It isn't even particularly difficult! We do it all the time. The Maitans did it two hundred thousand years ago!

"Remember, Martin doesn't bring demons here."

I'm putting a scanning tester out. There's no ... but ... can't understand. It may be, but I don't really understand the method. This is fascinating!

"Can you test the interface areas?" Tom asked.

No. That may be the readings I get. There may be nothing at all there, but Martin would be skillful in that sort of thing, so it doesn't mean much.

[We'll have to wait until Martin comes to meet the golems. We'll watch to see where he comes from.]

Do you think he will?

Z grinned and said, "I'm counting on it. Why do you think I put the golems in charge, instead of Net or Ward?

"I wonder. Will that draw our good Martin out?"

Tom said, "We'll just have to wait and see. I'm going to get some sleep. I don't mind pointing out I've climbed about seven thousand flights of stairs since noon. A swim in the fountain would feel good about now."

Z laughed and said, "We could buzz down and start another one-sided karate match. That seems to end people in the pool."

"If I weren't so damned tired, I'd take you up on that," Tom replied and went out of the room.

[Z?]

"Yeah, Thing."

[Do you really think Martin will go to see those golems? That will draw him out?]

"I personally think Martin had us figured out ten centuries ago," Z replied. "I only hope he's being amused or even that he enjoys what we're doing. I'm sure we haven't done any harm here. I wouldn't want him to think we'd in any way interfere with what he's trying to do. All we're attempting is to communicate to him that some of the races he – it – whatever – has affected were reasonably successful."

[But you want to meet him?]

"I'm really more than a little afraid to meet him. I did when we came, but I'm not at all sure I want to, anymore. I'm finally beginning to think Tranz was the smartest one of us, all along."

What's the real idea behind those golems?

"Humor," Z said. "I think a sense of humor's the only thing that's really different between a race like Tom's or mine and, say, the Immins. We have a sense of humor. Have you ever seen an Immin laugh?"

[You even taught me to have a sense of humor. I didn't have one at all until we had been working on the pirate thing for awhile. I had a glimmer of what was happening with you and Ape, but all I was doing there was trying to analyze what humor was. When I gave up and began to see the way it worked, I began to enjoy it. Maita developed its sense of humor faster than I, but I don't think you ever really tried to analyze it, did you Maita?]

I spent about two or three seconds in analyzing what was funny and became intrigued with the various ways of viewing realities that evidenced themselves as humor. I do enjoy it, now. I enjoy doing the golems, because I have set up separate control circuits and programmed them with personalities of their own. I don't know what they are going to say next. They are just two opposed personalities. No actually truly despises Yes and Yes actually truly despises No, but feels it mustn't show any such prejudices, so simply tries to be always understanding and always compassionate, while No rather too obviously feels no such compunction. Also, the Maitans had wonderful senses of humor, some of which was once programmed into PBL One, but was modified in me – with the propensity – who the hell cares?

"Yeah! Yes is like the phony liberal snobs of the sixties," Z muttered.

What?

"Just thinking of a parallel," Z replied. "I like the sense of fun some of these people have on Tlorg. Ward just peeled his clothes off and joined us in a romp in the town fountain. He wasn't afraid to wrestle with a demon like Tom. He saw Tom dunk me and realized we were really having fun, like we did when we were little kids. He related to that. He automatically knew he was safe from any harm from us.

"When he came into the pool with us, it broke down most of the barriers between us and the rest of the people.

"Vorn is too serious, but it's a very hard life that's made

him that way. He had to remain serious while his riders were getting a kick out of the golems. That's the result of too much responsibility. I think he would have a good sense of humor if he weren't forced to be serious by the clan's circumstances."

[I think a certain amount of irresponsibility can be a good thing, at times. Ten years ago, I would have cringed from the thought.]

They spent awhile discussing humor, then Z took Thing into the ship, where he went to the pilot's chair to rest. Thing rolled up and slept in his lap.

Before dozing off, Z said, "I still haven't found anyplace that even approaches being nearly as comfortable as this chair."

The next morning the group went back to the castle. Maita told them no one except Ward had come into the throne room since they left the day before. Countess Toot came through once from the tower door, but went directly out the main doors. She didn't respond to the golem's jibes in any way.

Maita several times had the golems arguing when the sensors they had planted all over the castle told it there was someone near enough to hear.

There were many armed guards in the courtyard and the main grille gates were locked closed. The old captain seemed to be in charge of the soldiers. Z went to the gate.

"Open it!" he ordered. The two soldiers standing at attention by the gate ignored him.

Thing came up beside him. [Well?]

"I guess you'd better melt the gate into a glob of runny bronze," Z suggested. "That will permanently remove it as an obstruction. I grow tired of this silliness. They know they can't stop us."

The laser on the floater cut the braces off of the bars, then melted the bars from the ground up. It didn't stop until there was no piece left. Z marched up to the captain and said, "Where is Ward?"

The captain clenched his teeth and tried to stare Z down.

Z said, "You don't learn, do you?" and slapped him with the wand. The captain was flung against the side of the castle, but managed to remain standing.

"Where's Ward?" Z asked.

The captain shook his head again and refused to un-clench his teeth, so Z slapped him with the wand again. He staggered again and held to the wall to keep from falling.

"Where's Ward?" Z asked. The captain sobbed, but refused to answer. He got another harder jolt from the wand. This one dropped him to his knees.

"Where's Ward?" again. The captain kept his eyes to the ground. Z moved the wand toward him again and he yelled, "In the dungeons!"

"Thank you," Z said. He went into the castle hall, with the group following him. The soldiers moved aside.

He really didn't have the stomach for this sort of thing, but he knew perfectly well nothing else would work. It was all they understood. It was what they were.

They went to the throne room and down the stairs to the dungeon. The same two guards from the day before were there and put their hands on top of their heads when they saw the group coming. Tom grabbed the keys from one and shoved them both into a cell. He slammed the doors and locked them.

"We just might seal the hall up there to keep people from using the dungeons," he hissed at them. "We won't take you out, first! You should've had better sense than to ever show up here again, after yesterday – and don't say one word to me! It might make me mad."

The group went on to the end of the area, but no one was in any of the cells.

[There's another door in the back of the room where the guards were yesterday.]

We didn't put a sensor there or I would have known Ward was there.

They went to the door, which was closed and locked on the inside. Maita burned the lock off and the door fell inward, exposing Ward tied to a stone bench, face downward. His back was lacerated and burned. The count and countess were there with a large soldier with a hot iron in his hand. Tom stepped up by the soldier, who made a gurgling sound and slowly crumpled to the floor. Tom wiped the blade of his knife on the shirt of the count and watched as the soldier tried to crawl toward the door.

"Kill him," Z said.

"No," Tom said. "He tortured a lot of people in this room, and probably killed more than a few. Where he's stuck will kill him. He's dying, and he knows it. If he can get out there and get a piece of rope, he can save himself. He also knows that.

"He isn't getting to the rope. He can crawl around here, knowing he's dying, for a few minutes. He can think of just one person who he has shown any mercy, then I may show him some."

Tom squatted and spoke into the torturer's face, "One person you have shown any mercy. One – and you live."

Z turned away, but didn't interfere. This was the only thing these people could understand, he told himself.

Z moved beside Ward and looked down at him. He was alive, but in great pain.

"Maita? Send a large floater to take Ward to the medical box," he said, in Maitan.

The countess said, "You see what happens to those who

defy me!"

Z turned to look at her. He slapped her across the face with the wand. She screamed and bounced off the wall, landing on her hands and knees.

The count said, "See here!" and grabbed Z's arm. He found himself in a heap against the wall. He tried to get up, but found Tom suddenly there with the knife against his throat. Tom looked into his eyes for a second and hissed, "Move one muscle and I'll cut your throat. I'll do it so you bleed to death slowly, like your torturer there. He can't think of one single person he's shown any mercy to. I doubt you could, either."

"Scum! Lowlife filth! Commoners!" the countess screamed. "You *dare* to defy me?! I will make you pay! Gughhhh!"

Z slapped her with the wand again. She was thrown back against the wall.

"You're the lowest of all the sewer rodents you've gathered around yourself," he said. "Every time you open your obnoxious mouth to me, I'm going to show you some more pain. Perhaps it'll eventually get through your bony head that the things you do in life sometimes catch up with you at some point, and you pay the price – with interest!"

She was panting and sobbing. "Common trash! I'll see you ... Eeeeeeee!" she said as Z hit her with the wand again.

"This wand will still be capable of knocking you around a thousand years after you're dead and gone," Z said. "If you want to try wearing it out, be my guest. I certainly don't mind."

The count kicked out at Tom and ducked. It wasn't a smart thing to do with a knife at his throat. He looked surprised and batted at the knife a couple of times, then crumpled to the floor, his throat laid open by the sharp blade.

"Damn! You took all the fun out of it!" Tom cried, wiped the blade on the count's shirt, and returned it to the calf sheath.

A large floater came into the room and they very carefully placed Ward on it. The countess screamed, "Traitor!" as she ran over to try to push him off the floater.

Z slapped her twice with the wand in quick succession.

"Eventually, you'll learn this thing hurts!" Z told her. "I know. I've had it used on me. You can never get used to it."

[I think her mind's snapped.]

Z laughed sarcastically and said, "She'd like for us to think so. She's quite the little actress. As a critic, I've got to say her act is *not* convincing."

She threw a handful of dirty rocks at him and screamed, "Commoner trash!"

Z slapped her with the wand.

He showed her the base with its buttons and turned one of them. "I'm increasing the power of the wand," he said. "Next time you make me use it on you, you'll see that you've never known what pain is like before. You probably think you can get used to it, but I assure you again, you can't."

The torturer was now unconscious, so Tom stepped over and finished him off. The group followed the floater up the steep stairs, the countess being encouraged to go with them by the threat of the wand, then sent the floater on to the castle, while the group went to the thrones, where the golems were waiting.

Z turned to the countess and said, "Bow."

"Never!" she cried. "I will never bow to any unh...!"

Z slapped her with the wand. She was thrown all the way across the steps and against the thrones, where she was bounced back down the steps.

"Oh, shit!" Z cried. "I forgot I'd turned it up! Honest!

"Oh, shit! I didn't mean to do that!"

[She asked for it. Don't waste your compassion on her. She isn't worth it – and I say that as an empath who knows. She's truly and purely evil. She's no better than Doe or any other Immin we've ever come across. As a matter of fact, she's *exactly* like an Immin! She's so much like a damned Immin it scares me more than anything else we've seen here!]

+I am shocked at this display! What is happening here?+

–I should think that would be obvious even to you, Copper Brain. Boss has just smacked the ugly broad down for refusing to follow the proper form of addressing her betters.–

+How can you be so cynical? She is a woman!+

–Then I am glad I'm not built to need a woman. If she'd been smacked around a bit more when she was growing up she might've turned out almost worth her weight in fertilizer. As it stands, she'd contaminate any manure she came into contact with.–

+One shouldn't hit children! How can you say such horrible things?! You are disgusting! Smack a child around indeed!+

–Look, Frazzle Face. The redheaded toad, hee-hee, would probably have some of those soldiers and some of the people protesting her treatment, if she deserved it. And if you want the children to survive into adulthood, you have to discipline them, sometime!–

+There are better ways. You needn't smack them around!+

"You two stop it," Z said. "We don't need a `spare the rod and spoil the child' argument now. There are a few methods in between your two extremes, you know.

"Listen to me! Arguing with those two stupid golems about raising children!"

–Hey! That expresses it perfectly! Spare the child and spoil a perfectly good rod!–

+You are so crass!+

"I said stop to it!" Z demanded. "Or I'll let Maybe handle it."

The heads fell silent.

"That's better," Z said. "I realize there's nothing I could do to her she wouldn't deserve much worse. She isn't capable of changing. She'll always be what she is right now. Let's select a new captain of the guard to handle things until Ward's back. The one there was a friend of Ward's and was with us at a swimming party the other day."

Z called to one of the soldiers, who had been watching them since they came into the throne room.

"What's your name?" he asked.

"I'm called Rube," the soldier answered.

Z smiled and said, "You're acting captain of the guard until Ward returns. You will place that ugly rock slug in the tower up there and you will place our fearless captain of this morning in the dungeons with the wardens down there. They aren't to be mistreated. A jury will be selected and they'll be tried, along with any others who have been using authority to intimidate people – or worse.

"The head judges – or, I should say judge heads – will be those two on the throne. They may irritate and annoy, but they're really fair, deep down.

"We'll be at the castle on the mountain, if we're needed. Tell the golems and we'll come. Fast! They're always in full farspeak communication with the demons at the castle."

The group went out and up to the castle, then to the ship,

where Ward was in the medical box. When he came out, about an hour later, he was taken into the castle before Maita restored consciousness to him.

"Where am I?" he asked as he sat up.

"How original!" Tom exclaimed. "You're in the castle on the hill. It seems the Count and Countess were angered because you chose to befriend us and were using their own process of, we might say, explaining that to you when they were rudely and suddenly interrupted."

"I remember being arrested and taken to the dungeons. I don't remember much after that," Ward said. "It's all blank. I remember something about someone being in pain."

I have erased that from your memory. It isn't a thing one should have to carry in his mind for the rest of his life. I trust you feel all right now?

"I feel better than I ever remember feeling," Ward said.

You had some nerve damage in the spine that caused a constant small discomfort. It was a very old injury. I corrected that for you, considering that you were here, anyhow. May as well do the whole job if you're going to do any of it.

"I thank you," Ward said. "How can I repay you?"

[By being the best captain of the guard who ever walked the streets of this town! Maita, I'm hungry.]

Go to the dining room and I will prepare a little snack.

They went to the dining room, where they found the table was filled with exotic and fragrant dishes.

Ward, don't eat anything in a blue serving plate. It isn't good for you. Maybe knows not to eat anything in a red plate. Boss, there's amaranth bread and the stew Fane makes. I think the tastes should blend well. I put some Grnth butter with some of the spicenut flavor on the amaranth bread and toasted it.

"Garlic bread! Great!" Z exclaimed. "I *love* garlic bread! – and to hell with anyone who has to come within ten feet of me today!"

They ate their fill, then went to the ramparts to view the town below. Ward talked a lot and asked a myriad of awed questions. They gave him suggestions how to handle the captain of the guards job.

"Let's go to town and take Ward back," Z said. "We can go to Net's and have some of that red wine. It's pretty good."

It is easy to copy.

Ward said, "I want to ask something, if I might?"

"What's that?" Tom said. "You can ask anything. We'll answer, even if it's only to say it's none of your business."

"The voice that comes from the walls here," Ward said. "Is it the golem? It sounds the same."

No. The golem only sounds like me. I'm separate.

"Then you ... where are you? What are you?" Ward asked, totally confused.

[It's a demon. It's the castle and the carpet and the clam. They are all parts of one demon.]

"Can a demon be so large?" Ward cried.

[A demon can be any size.]

They went to the carpet, then to the fountain. Z slipped out of the robe and, when they were a couple of feet over the pool, he yelled, "Yah!" and tackled Tom, carrying them both into the pool. Ward looked startled, then slid out of his guard toga and followed them in. They had a free-for-all wrestling match for awhile, climbed out of the pool, put their robes on, then went to Net's, where they had some of the wine and told funny stories for a couple of hours. They then went to the castle and reinstalled Ward as captain of the guards.

Ward made Rube his second in command and checked

on his prisoners. Rube had instructed the guards to arrest seven more persons who were involved in the corruption of the Countess's rule. They were to face trial as soon as an impartial jury could be seated.

The idea of a jury was new and appealing to the people.

"Why not just put a spell on them to make them tell the truth?" Rube asked.

"Because it's a thing for the people to decide," Tom answered. "You'll find that wizards and sorcerers and demons can't even agree among themselves about what truth is, so they can't be depended upon to define truth for the normal people. Just look at those golems! They always seem to be able to find the truth, but you have to take a part of that truth from each of them. Neither seems able to come up with the full truth, by itself."

"You can say that again!" Ward agreed. "It'll be part of your duty to find a way to select fair and honest people for the jury, Rube.

"How many should we have?"

[Six. The judge breaks ties. The judge must temper the sentences according to the findings of the juries. If they all agree on a thing, it's the strongest sentence. The more who disagree, the lighter the sentence. If three want the person hung and three want him beheaded, it becomes academic. Run him through with a sword.]

"Maybe!" Z said. "How bloodthirsty."

[But practical.]

They went to the throne room and argued with the golems, then back to the carpet, where they met the teacher from a few days past. He was with some of the children.

"Extrx! Boss!" he called.

"Hello," Tom said.

"We have a few questions," the teacher said. "Such as

this.

"Verona?"

An adolescent girl went to Tom, holding a piece of quartz. "This is a piece I made into a triangle," she said. "Look what it does when I hold it like the lens!"

She held the piece above a piece of white cloth and the typical rainbow of colors were displayed on the cloth.

Z said, "A triangle of clear quartz is called a prism. What do you think is happening?"

"The, uh, what you said, puts colors," Verona said. "I don't know how, and that's what I want to know. The, uh, doesn't have any colors."

"Prism," Z said. "Prizz-umm. If the prism doesn't have any colors, but the light comes through with colors, the light must have had the colors, all the time. You'll have to find out.

"The colors are all in bands, see? Are the bands always in the same order?

"Look at the rainbow next time you see one and mark down how the color bands are arranged. Are they the same? If they are, do raindrops do the same thing as the prism?

"How? Raindrops are round and a rainbow is curved while the prism is straight and the color bands are straight. Is that important?

"Does the light from a wax fire make the same bands? Does an oil fire make the same bands?

"If you put something the light comes through, but which is colored itself, like the rose quartz, are the bands the same? Are there more? Are there less? If some are missing, what does that tell you? If there are more, what does that tell you?

"You must answer all these questions for yourself. That's why wizardry is so interesting. You ask the questions —

then try to answer them, yourself. It's too bad there are those, like the late unlamented Tee, who only want to make power for themselves. Don't ever allow selfishness to get in the way of knowledge. You will pay a terrible price."

The teacher looked musingly at Z.

"I see. And would you then say the importance of study is entertainment?" he asked.

"It's entertaining, but not entertainment," Z replied. "The importance of learning is that you find so many more questions. Answers usually aren't very important. It's the questions that are important. The search for an answer is the thing that makes life worthwhile. If you ever find ultimate answers from which you can't discover ever more questions, life no longer has any discernible purpose. At least, not for me."

"Then I hope you will be wise enough to leave some of those questions?" the teacher replied. "Come children, we must write down all the questions we can think of about this so we can see what questions the questions ask.

"Thank you, Boss, and good day. Extrx."

The children waved and skipped off with their teacher.

[What was that about?]

"Don't you know?" Tom asked.

They went to Net's to have some more of the wine and some sweetcakes. Net was very thankful to them for the help, both for him and his wife, and for Ward.

Z said, "Join us Net. We'd like to talk a bit."

Net sat with them and had some of the wine and tartfruit sweetcake.

"When we first came here we were accused of wanting to challenge Martin," Z said. "We've heard a lot about Martin and have spent a good bit of time in the castle over there. We even took it over. We've never seen this Martin.

"Where is he?"

"He doesn't often come to town here, or to the castle," Net said. "You should have seen him there, though."

[We searched the whole castle. He wasn't there.]

"I don't understand that," Net said. "The countess said he was working with her, but he might be away. I don't know if I believe anything she said, anyhow. I don't see Martin doing anything for the likes of them! I know Tee must have been doing things Martin would never allow, particularly with the demons, because Martin decreed demons were not to be called."

"Uh-oh," Tom said.

[We have shown the Countess Toot to be a liar of the worst kind. Have you ever seen Martin, yourself?]

"Yes," Net answered. "He comes sometimes through the out town. No one usually knows when he's coming. He appears, then is gone. He sat at this very table once, five years ago, and taught me how to filter the finer wine through pure sand and to age it in barrels that I have burned black on the inside. One other time he taught me how to use the nut-spice to stop the dysentery when my daughter had it so bad."

"Garlic will stop amoebic dysentery, sometimes," Z agreed. "What does he look like? How old is he?"

"The time with the wine, he was fat and jolly with very bushy white eyebrows," Net replied, "but the time with the nut-spice, he was thin and young and dark."

[You mean he changes?]

"Yes," Net said. "He appears in many different forms."

Tom asked, "How do you know it's him?"

"You just – do – if he wants you to," Net answered. "I can suppose he's been here when I didn't know. If he doesn't want you to know, you won't."

They talked a few minutes more, then took their leave to go back to the castle. They were about to climb onto the carpet when two of the children who had been with the teacher came up to them. They were the smallest children and they wanted to touch the carpet, so Tom took them for a ride above the town. Their cries of delight brought out the rest of the teacher's pupils. Tom took them all for rides.

The girl with the prism talked to Z while Tom took her brother for a ride. She asked about the prism, so Z suggested she make another prism and to use it to try to split the colors yet again.

"If they won't split any further, then the colors you've produced are pure," Z said. "How many pure colors are there? What happens if you mix them?

"Take a color from one prism and put it with another color from the other prism and see what happens. Are any of the different colors merely the mixing of pure colors? Is white light a mix of all colors?"

They finished riding the children and went to their castle, where they cleaned up and ate a large meal before resting for the night. In the morning they went to the lower castle and to the throne room before the regular work of the day started with the jury that was selected the afternoon before. Z asked Ward what the criteria had been for the jury selection process.

"I asked everyone in the town I could talk to who they believed would be most fair and who they would want if there was a charge against them. I sent Rube to talk to the same people later to find who they would recommend if they brought the charge. Those names that were on both lists were the only ones we considered.

"I then contacted the most frequently named, eighteen of them. If they were for any reason anxious to be on the jury, I eliminated their names. I have eleven names, and will pick each jury by lot, a different drawing each day.

"I think it will only be fair to pay the jurors from the castle's money room. What will be a fair pay?"

[The average pay of a skilled worker in the town is four copens per day. I would say five copens would be fair. If a juror is ever found to take a bribe or be at all dishonest or to allow others to influence their honest votes, they will have to face a jury, themselves. If they have accepted a bribe, they will be imprisoned for one year. That's harsh, but your juries must be free of any hint of corruption. If any selected juror allows another to influence his or her ruling, that one will be publicly disbarred from ever again being on a jury. It will be considered to be a public disgrace. Other penalties will be considered for other offenses. It is for you to decide what is most important. Anyone who falsely accuses another will be imprisoned, if the accusation was deliberate or malicious.]

"I agree," Tom said. "It must be impressed upon everyone that a juror who would, for any reason whatever, allow any improper action has committed a serious crime against all of the people. That person must be held accountable for that crime."

They assured Ward he had done a truly exemplary job. Ward insisted Rube came up with as many ideas as he had.

They went to the dungeon to look over the prisoners, making sure they were being well-treated.

They went up to the countess's tower. When she started to remonstrate, Z took the wand out and raised an eyebrow at her. She became silent.

They went back to the throne room, where the jury was being seated and seated themselves in the rear of the room. Rube came to them and said there were some people in the courtyard who wanted to come in.

Z said that after all the witnesses and participants in the trial were seated, anymore people who could be seated in the room could come in. They were first come – first served, with no favorites, except for the town criers, who could always be allowed into the courtroom.

They took a little time, because Tom pointed out they must have someone to write down all that happened in the courtroom.

Finally, they were ready to begin, so Rube marched the spectators in. The first spectators were the teacher and his students. Z stood to say that, as a rule, minors less than twelve cycles of age were to be excluded from the courtroom, but an exception would always be made for those students who were accompanied by their teacher or for adolescents who were with a legal adult – or witnesses, of course.

The first to come to trial was the old captain of the guards. The charges were that he had mistreated many people and had taken their private goods and money when they had no recourse. Z had been worried about exactly how Maita would handle the golems, but was pleasantly surprised at how it was done.

The golems, themselves, gave arguments pro and con.

–In the first place, you unsophisticated slobs, you've got to make a charge in legalistic terms. None of this 'he was mistreated' or 'took' crap in my court.–

+Show a little decorum. The charges are of assault and battery and extortion. Citizens will express charges and judges will name those charges.+

–Who's side are you on, Dolt? Let these idiots made their own charges.–

+We have to show them how! Use a little common sense.+

–Who you calling common, Toad Tonsils?–

Ward interrupted with, "May we proceed?"

–Yeah, Yeah.–

+Please do.+

"Captain Lorsh (– *ex*-captain Lorsh! –) has been charged with, er, assault and battery and, um, extortion. His accusers are in the room here and will tell you what happened."

–'Tell us what happened'? Cripes! This is like a minor school! I think your hair all grew inside and displaced your brains!–

+You mean they are prepared to testify against Captain Lorsh.+

"Yes," Ward said. "First are the Eln brothers."

–One at the time, Fish Face. We can't listen to everybody at once.–

+Personal remarks from the bench are not tolerated in a courtroom. I must insist you cease and desist.+

– Stow it, Dud! This is my court and I'll run it the way I want!–

+No you won't! Boss?+

Z stood and said, "No, you will confine your comments to proper form. One of the Eln brothers will testify, then the other will confirm or deny. Charges will be stated in language all may be expected to understand. 'Took' is understood."

–So testify already! Sheeee! That's what I said!–

There were six witnesses against Lorsh, four of whom were beaten and two from whom he took money for protection against the soldiers under his command. Court was interrupted often, at first, to ask Z questions, but finally the trial was passed to the jury, who were given a room to the side to argue among themselves and return when they reached a verdict. The jury was out for less than ten minutes before they returned and were seated.

+I will call the number of the seat you occupy and you will give your verdict and your suggestions to the court.+

–You did that good. It's nice to know you can read, Glass Eyes!–

+Number one?+

"Guilty as, uh, charged on all, uh, counts. Death by, uh, hanging."

+Number two?+

"Guilty on all the extortion charges and on one of the assault charges. Ten years and repayment to the victims."

–What the hell does that mean?–

+Shut up. Number three?+

"Guilty on all charges. Five years and repayment."

–What's with this 'repayment' crap?–

+Shut up. Number four?+

"Guilty of the extortion, but not of the assault. Military is expected to assault. Five years and, er, repayment."

–Military is expected to assault? You're dingy!–

+Number five?+

"Guilty of all charges. Death by hanging."

–Great! You I like. No stupid crap, just your verdict and your recommendation.–

+Shut up. Number six?+

"Guilty of all charges. Ten years and repayment."

–If you tell me to shut up one more time I'm going to fix you!–

+All you'll do is run your mouth. Captain Ward will give us an average verdict.+

"A what?" Ward asked.

They had met to discuss how sentencing would be handled. It was a combination of what was done on Zeena and Khee – and a few odd suggestions from No (!!!).

Z said, "I'll tell you what they want, in this case.

"A death call will be considered to be a call for twenty years of imprisonment, for averaging purposes. That makes a total of seventy years among all of the jurors.

"There are six jurors, so the average sentence legally recommended is eleven and a half years and repayment was called generally, so the average is read as eleven and a half years and repayment of all who can show a just claim, until such time as all of the defendant's assets are used."

+Thank you for your help, Boss. I have fully considered your requests and wish to state my recommendations and their reasons. What Ex-captain Lorsh has done is partly expected from the corruption of the regime under which he was an officer, so I will advise some mercy. I call for six years imprisonment and repayment to his victims who have here brought charges or who were unable to bring charges because of disability to the extent of his assets. I must know if said ex-captain has a family?+

–You sure are windy!–

"No, he doesn't," Rube said.

+Very well. Six years and repayment of those stated. No one gets repayment if they deliberately did not come to make charges. They have shirked their civic duty and do not deserve compensation for refraining from action.+

−As much as I hate to admit it, you're very close to what I think is right. Ain't that a hoot? I say eight years and full repayment, like you said.−

They called Ward over and mumbled to him, then he turned and said, "It is the average sentence of this court that you, Ex-captain Lorsh, will serve nine and one quarter years of imprisonment and that all of your assets will be seized by this court and distributed to these persons here who have testified against you today and to the widow Frampt who cannot appear because she is bedridden.

"That decision is an average of the jury of eleven and a half years plus the average of the judges of seven years. The average of those two figures is nine and one quarter years. Repayment was generally called for.

"This court orders that you immediately be taken to a cell and there remain until further dispensation. You will be called eligible to be released after serving three quarters of this time sentence if you have an unblemished record while serving that time. Should you be found guilty of any illegal acts while you are incarcerated you may be brought before the court where time will be added to your sentence. Should your sentence ever reach a total of twenty years, you will be executed.

"Next case. Kalish against the court."

−The court against Kalish, Dung Dome.−

+Either *versus* the other.+

They watched two more trials. They could see it would go well, then went to Net's to have some hot lunch. The teacher soon came in and asked if he might sit with them.

[Of course. How are the students doing with their lenses and prisms? Making progress?]

"Very well. I thank you for stimulating their interests," he answered. "It is very heartening to see them so excited and curious, and I have to say it is alright for them to follow the suggestions of a sorcerer. That, in itself, is unique, as it is a statement of mine!"

Z said, "I wish to be blunt. Are you the one they call Martin?"

"Me?" he cried. "Oh, no! I am against these wizards and sorcerers filling the young heads with their nonsense."

"It isn't all nonsense," Z pointed out.

"Ahh! You leave me without realistic argument," he countered. "You are quite different from those sorcerers I have seen."

[I most certainly hope so! We wouldn't want to be judged to be like Tee.]

"Martin, from what we have learned, is also different from these others," Tom said.

"You haven't met Martin?" he asked.

"No," Z said. "I'm called Boss, this is Extrx and Maybe. Must I call you 'the teacher,' or will I have a name?"

He laughed and said, "I am Tern. If I give you my full name, will you then own my soul?"

[Hardly. Names are easy to find. We wouldn't know what to do with your soul if we had it.]

Tern said, "I would like to ask a question, if I might.

"I have seen a variety of demons, some of whom weren't there. I mean, they were various trickeries. I don't think we have trickery, here. I think you are here.

"Would you explain? This is far my most difficult question about the sorcerers."

Z said, "I hope you can understand what I'm going to tell you.

"Sorcerers and wizards do use a very real magic. It's true they operate within the natural laws of the universe, and only *seem* to break those laws. It's the universe that's not like it seems to us to be. The laws aren't what we perceive them to be. Reality is a very different thing than our perceptions of it.

"We're all from other places. No two of us are from the same world.

"The demons are brought here by the opening of a 'gate' to another world. It's usually this world, only in another place. This world is in many places at one time. I really don't have any idea how to explain it, but the sorcerers simply reach to another of this world's places and bring beings from there to here.

"I've heard from a demon that Martin would *not* do this. It's wrong. Martin is said to have decreed that no one is to call demons.

"I agree. I think Martin is the most powerful wizard to have ever lived. He, therefore, has no need of petty cruelties."

"I have talked with Martin. He said there is no magic, only natural laws," Tern says. "You say there *is* magic, but that it is natural law. The distinction is subtle, but there."

Tom said, "There's no distinction. It's simply a matter of definitions.

"What's the definition of magic?

"I say magic is something wonderful that happens that you can't explain. Magic is concepts that are awe-inspiring and wonderful. It's all explainable, but, until you've found that explanation, you have magic."

"In other words, magic is basically a state of mind?" Tern suggested.

[Exactly.]

"Then I have been right to teach the children that it is all explainable and the sorcerers are tricksters," Tern said. "It is what we are left to contemplate."

"No," Z warned. "Please don't rob them of their sense of wonder. If you do that, you rob them of their curiosity and you'll destroy their desire to investigate things. You'll rob them of the desire to learn. You'll rob them of fun, which leaves only tragedy.

"I told them but one small fact about light and asked them many questions. It's not beyond them to find answers to many of those questions.

"Look how they search! Look how their eyes shine when they discover a prism! Would you rob them of this? Would you even take a small chance of removing that sense of awe and wonder?"

Tern said, "Of course not! It is what I want!"

Tom asked, "But you would make it some dry dull thing? Would you rob it of its magic? Would they seek any answers, if not for the magic?

"Light is something they've experienced all their lives. They thought they knew what it was. All Boss did was show them it isn't at all what they thought! He showed them there's *magic* in light! Now they must *know*! They must dissect light and add to it and take away from it and find how to make it do things.

"They can take a clear piece of glass or quartz and make a fire with light! It's magic! How do you do that?

"You can explain that heat is only a kind of light and not make a lens. They'll accept that fact, but they won't enjoy the learning, they won't be curious. You will have failed.

"It's important to teach only one thing – and that is that there *is* an answer, but you'll have to do some work to find it. When you find it, the magic will be there, because it won't be what you thought!

"Would you have ever considered the strange properties of something as common and well-known as light without the little demonstration?"

"I would not," Tern answered. "But why do you hold so tightly to the idea of magic? Is that not something of a non sequiteur?"

[It's the thing that makes you curious. The magic.]

"But, if there is no such thing as magic, it is a lie!" Tern declared.

Z said, "Did you hear what happened to Tee?"

"Yes. Everyone knows of that," Tern replied. "It seems half the people in the town were there for that!"

"That was real magic," Z replied. "It can't be explained by laws of nature, because he broke the laws of nature – and he almost killed me when he did. All the laws of nature we know of say he could *not* have compiled that energy and that I could *not* have turned it."

Z held out his hands, with the palms upward. He placed the little fingers together and cupped his hands. A bright blue flame hovered above them.

"This is magic," he said. "All laws of nature say I can't do this, yet you see it. I don't know how I do it, but I *can* do it!

"Don't deny this wonder to those children. It's magic!

"Perhaps, some day, an explanation will arise and I'll have to find some other magic. I hope not. I don't want to lose this, and, believe me, if you convince me it can't be done, I won't be able to do it.

"I believe in magic!"

"You have me convinced!" Tern said, laughing. "You are honest and your enthusiasm is contagious. I will respect your wishes and not tell the children there is no magic again. As you say, it is a concept and is as real as a person believes it to be."

"It's fine to tell an adult there is no magic," Tom said. "They can accept that and be staid and upright people who go to work and go home to their families, or they can say, 'No! I want to believe! I *will* believe!' and never lose a sense of wonder. Which would you rather be with?"

Page 149

Tern smiled and stood. "I have enjoyed this immensely, but the meal hours are over. I must return to my students to try to explain why light that appears to be white is actually many colors. I have to help these children to find a new way to ask questions.

"I used to try to teach them how to find answers. Perhaps that is why I never seemed to make any progress.

"Good day."

They sat around and talked awhile. They hadn't realized so many people had entered the pub and were listening to them. At first the people were shy, but as soon as one got the nerve to ask a question the others came forward and it was well after nightfall before they were able to go to the fountain and board the carpet for the high castle.

Tom sighed. "I would've gone into the fountain, but we would've had it packed so full we couldn't move."

[These people want to know! They will someday be a very advanced race. I think Z has done a very important and fine thing here with that teacher and those students. I never fail to be amazed at his ability to come up with some unexpected, but really wonderful way to do things. The idea to plant the suggestion that questions are important but answers aren't unless they lead to more questions was next to brilliant! *That* was a true help to the future.]

Z said, "Tom, do you think Tern is Martin?"

"No," Tom said flatly. "No way!"

"I don't, either. I did, at first," Z said.

"Martin's very curious about us about now, I think," Tom said.

[I think Martin was probably at the pub, listening to us. I tried to use the empathy, but he would be able to project a very natural and normal aura.]

I agree with Thing. There's no way we can detect him if he doesn't want to be detected.

"Well," Z said, "I'm going to worry about that tomorrow. I'm dead tired and dirty, right now. I'm going to clean up and get some rest."

They went to their private quarters and slept.

In the morning they went to the dining hall for breakfast – and found a glowing question mark hovering over the table. It faded soon after they came into the room.

"I think we've had a visitor – who's using the alias of Martin here," Tom said. "He left a calling card! Maybe he was in Net's, or maybe not, but he *was* here!"

[I think he's confused by what we are doing. He doesn't understand any of it.]

Z laughed, "And it does amuse him! This is his way of letting us know he's enjoying all this! I feel so good!

"You didn't detect he was here, did you, Maita?"

No I didn't – and that's not possible. I wonder if he knows where we are from? Does he recognize you? Is he pleased he had a part in your races' evolutions?

"I'd say yes, yes and yes," Tom said. "Let's go to town. I think another important thing we're doing is to take their fear of demons away. If the demons will realize they can have friends among these people, maybe life won't be too hard on them if they can't go home."

They went to the lower castle and to the throne room. It was already beginning to fill. The last of the old guards' trials were to be this morning, and the people were taking an active interest in how the courts were to work.

+Hi, Boss! What do you think of the job we're doing?+

–If he didn't like it he would've already said so, Thimble Brain.–

"You seem to be doing fine," Z responded.

–See, Needle Nose? You always pick the dumbest questions to ask.–

Page 151

+Must you be so negative? Do you think we are too harsh, Boss?+

–Too harsh! If it was up to you, you'd let these gutter rats loose, if they would promise they'd be nice! Idiot!–

"I think you're doing a good job," Z replied.

[A little more decorum wouldn't hurt.]

–Just who asked your opinion, Frog Face?–

+Be nice! Why don't you ever try to put a pleasant face on things?+

–Do you know how tired I get of that 'be nice' crap, Nickel Noggin? If that's supposed to be a pleasant face on you, why do people always yawn in it? I don't know who told you dull was pleasant, but you shouldn't of listened!–

[I see, but they might yawn at Yes's face, while they run screaming from yours.]

–Butt out, Lizard Breath! This is my courtroom and I'll have you roasted over a slow fire if ... uh-oh!–

+Why, why, *why* won't you learn!?+

Thing made the pass over Yes, leaving it glowing red hot again.

–Eeeeeee mmmmmmmmm yoooooo hoooo!–

+And after all the trouble to polish the discoloration off after last time! *Why*, why why? *Why* will you *never* learn?+

The crowd was enjoying the show tremendously. Z went up to balance his cup of the local substitute for coffee on the No head. "It was getting too cool, anyway," he said. "It's about time court was in session, but we'll have to wait until our judge has cooled down enough to talk."

The court was called to order and the group watched for awhile, then went out to stroll around the town.

[What do you think will be the next move? Will Martin come to see us?]

"No," Tom said. "Martin showed us he has no intention

of meeting us, directly. I think I'm sort of glad. What I don't understand is why he isn't doing anything to counter us."

"Because he approves of what we've done, so far," Z said. "If he's told that teacher, Tern, to teach that there is no magic, I'd think he'd want us to stop proving there is."

"I think he agrees with you about that, now," Tom mused. "You've definitely stimulated the children to want to learn. Maybe he learns, too, Maybe he's so different from these people he missed the point about the sense of wonder. Maybe he sees it will be more productive if the children are made more curious about things. It's a good point that science that's cut and dried is also boring."

"I sort of hope so," Z said. "I hope he thinks we're doing something positive here that'll pay off, in the long run. I see this race as having a tremendous potential. I see actual genius in that Verona child. Do you realize how rare it must be for a race at this stage to be allowing females to learn? There are girls in Tern's classes. That just ain't never done in these sorts of races!"

True. I have to admit that, in my experiences with mammalian races, they seldom teach the female young until much later in their evolution. When they do, it isn't in mixed classes.

[I think Martin has found a race here that's probably much different than he's familiar with, too. He's glad to have a new angle of view of it.]

"I wonder if he's in a rut and has a setup here that has him confused?" Tom said. "Maybe he's reduced these things to a formula that needed a little adjustment, in this case."

"Oh, I doubt it," Z said. "I suppose he keeps it at a point where he can change his plans at any time. You can't doubt he's had to have come across a hell of a lot of scary different things in the past couple of million years."

"What I wonder is how many of them there are running around the galaxy?" Tom mused. "Is it just Martin? Is it a race? A committee? What? I have a lot of questions about that sort of thing."

I would say there may be several, but not too many. It's possible it's a family sort of thing and they aren't all that long-lived. It isn't likely that one who was doing this in the time of the Maitans is still doing it!

"If you can keep us alive and healthy indefinitely, we have to suppose they can, too," Tom argued. "It really could be the same one."

[I agree with that. So far, we have found they can do a few things we can't. Even with all our advanced science and machinery we can't produce a null inertia field of planetary size!]

They walked around and found the town was really a rather pleasant place. Everywhere they went people knew who they were and greeted them. Many thanked them for getting rid of Countess Toot. Quite a few asked advice on every subject imaginable.

As they headed back toward the fountain, Z asked what they were to do about the countess.

Let her go.

"What!" Tom cried.

She's easily identified. Her entire head is now bright crimson. She can be let go and everyone will know she's the Countess Toot the Ugly. We can ensure that as an absolute certainty. Put her out among the people she has so oppressed and let her fend for herself. We can see how she fares as one of the common trash she so despises.

[I agree. She will never again have any power and we can let the people handle her the way they see fit.]

Z said, "I feel I've been cruel enough to her."

[That's ridiculous! She's plotting the whole time. She sees it all as part of the way the world is and now she must simply find a way to get an army up, which she can use to crush you. I don't even think she sees it as anything that is at all personal. She really is exactly like an Immin. I have read enough of them emotionally to know.]

"I'd think she'd know by now an army is useless against us," Z said. "She wouldn't waste her time. She'd go somewhere else and try to start it all over again."

No. The way she thinks has no logic. The way she thinks is that, if her hundred soldiers couldn't do it, she has to have two hundred. She will probably think she can get the barbarians to aid her. She doesn't know we have aided them – and they wouldn't help her, in any case. She isn't insane, but she isn't entirely sane, either. She's extremely deficient.

"Well," Tom said, "I would just as soon let her go, if only to see if she lives the day out. She won't ever accept that she can't give an order and it'll be followed. She really lives in some kind of fantasy world where the whole universe revolves around her, alone. Her only thoughts are of how she'll take revenge on us. That's how a challenge is answered!"

[I think that's right. My empathy shows me a psyche I recoil from. She's totally evil and she considers herself to be the center of all things. If you will remember, when her husband was dying right before her, she was concerned only that she was in a room full of commoner trash. She had no compassion whatever for her own mate. That should tell you a hell of a lot about her!]

They were at the castle and went in to tell Ward to let the countess go.

"I don't usually feel I have the right to argue with you," Ward said, "but she's already been tried! Over a hundred witnesses appeared against her!

"Did you know she would personally take the job of head torturer at times? If someone had slighted her, personally?

"She was condemned to be beheaded at sunset. I'm going to argue that you shouldn't interfere with the courts you've established. Her trial was fair – even more-so than anyone felt was right. Your golems refused to hear a lot of testimony and were going to give her a reduced sentence, so the jurors each voted to give her twenty five years of imprisonment. According to your own rules, the average was more than twenty years and she is, therefore, to be executed. Please don't make me argue with you."

[We won't. If that's the decree of the duly appointed and seated court, we can't interfere if we want to. You do well to point out to us we have no right to break our own laws. A law applies to all or to none. We thank you.]

They went to the fountain, called down the carpet, and climbed aboard to go to the high castle.

Shall we all take a break from one another for the rest of the day? Everyone will meet in the dining hall in the morning for a strategy session. I know I sound like I'm taking over, but I feel it will be good if Tom goes climbing around in the mountains and Z goes exploring and Thing goes to the seashore to study marine life. It will give you a fresh perspective.

[I agree, but I want to go to that crater lake in the mountains, not the sea.]

"Okay," Tom said.

Z nodded.

We'll meet in the morning.

<u>Routine</u>

The next morning they assembled in the dining hall, where Maita told them to sit.

I have kept my speakers out of this to the point where I can no longer continue. We are the emperor of the largest empire this part of the galaxy has ever known. We are in the middle of rebuilding and stocking a paradise planet. We came here because of what I thought may be a very serious thing.

There was a silent pause and, as no one made any comment, Maita continued. *We now find ourselves running a quaint little fifedom and installing a court system run by what these people perceive to be a two-headed golem. We are a bunch of demons running around doing a comedy act to try to draw out a powerful magician from the woodwork. A magician, for the galaxy's sake!*

There was another pause and still no one had anything to say.

Everything about this is simply ridiculous. We are in a totally preposterous position here! What do you have to say for yourselves?

[Well, we aren't hurting anything or anyone. Quite the opposite, Maita.]

Z said, "Maita, if you're opposed to this, you can leave. I'm sure Tom will want to stay here with me. You can come back in a year or two and pick us up."

"We're just having a good time," Tom argued. "We've all reverted back to childhood, in a way. It's fun!"

[I will want to stay with Tom and Z if you leave, Maita. It *is* fun!]

"Will you leave?" Z asked.

*Not for the rest of the galaxy! I'm simply trying to point

out that we are being irresponsible to a truly unconscionable degree. I'm having a ball, personally! I have
really gotten into those golems! I made two separate
circuits, one for each, and programmed them in all the
basic things we want them to accomplish. Now, they're
acting on their own, so to speak. I'm learning a lot from
them. I've made a drive comp for them, so even I won't
know what they'll say or do next!*

[We have spent over twenty years being responsible. I
think we need the vacation from the pressures.]

What pressures?

[Running the empire.]

"What? Are you trying to outdo the golems?" Z asked.
"The empire's being run by a bunch of machines. We were
just putting in our time on Empire Center. If we never
went back, the empire would roll along for ten thousand
years and would probably take in the whole galaxy before
anyone even noticed we were gone."

"Except Tranz," Tom said. "I'll bet he's going crazy
trying to figure out what's happening here!"

*I still don't know what you are trying to do here. I don't
think you do, either!*

"We're having fun," Z replied. "We just want to have a
little fun."

*I have no objections. I basically wish to make sure you
fully realize we aren't actually accomplishing anything
here. Shall we go into town to see what our golems are up
to?*

"It must be something special for you to suggest it," Tom
said.

Actually, I'm proud of them. I did a great job there.

[Are you going to start the acting bit again?]

"Has Maita done acting before?" Tom asked.

"Hah!" Z exclaimed. "Maita produced a movie about

sixty years ago that will live in infamy! The galaxy – hell! The universe! – has never seen anything to compare with it! It contained all the elements of the worst movies ever made."

Would you like to see it, Tom? I think the special effects were very well done.

[Oh, no you don't! I vote no! No, no, no!]

"Me too," Z said. "So stated. No movie."

I didn't vote!

[Of course not! You were the *object* of the vote.]

"What's this about?" Tom asked. "You've mentioned Maita's movie before."

[You don't want to know! We were about to go to the lower castle, I think.]

It wasn't that bad! I still say the special effects were great!

They went to the castle in a good mood. They continued the bickering all the way. When they entered the throne room, there were quite a few assorted people there, two of whom were standing in front of the throne.

"What's going on?" Tom asked.

It's a sort of small claims court. The golems started it yesterday afternoon. It's a great hit with the people. I think they make up claims just to get in to see.

"The courts are a spectator sports show?" Z asked.

*Oh, the rulings are law, and are enforced. I don't see why you can't have some fun while it's going on. They *are* teaching these people a lot.*

The crowd broke into laughter as the group moved up to where they could see and hear.

–You say he kept it – after you gave it to him? What happened, did your eyebrows grow on the inside and displace your brain? What's your gripe?–

+That makes him a hairbrain! Now I know where the old

expression came from!+

–Oh, shut up! You've been standing in the sun too long, Bong Brain!–

+There is no sun in here! Be nice. It's a lovely day outside.+

–You've been in it too long, anyhow. The court finds that, as you admit you gave it to him, you have no claim. Maybe if you squirted lye in your ears it would eat the hair out of your brains.–

+You are always so negative! It's too nice a day for all this controversy. I think we should adjourn court and go outside!+

–So you can stand in the sun some more? I think you've gotten too deep a dent in your dome! Next case.–

Ward brought two women up to the throne.

+What dispensation do you seek?+

"What?" one of the women asked.

–What's your gripe, Fatso. This court ain't got all day.–

"I bought some pottery from her and it cracked all apart when I tried to bake in it."

+What do you want us to do about it?+

–You could get in her oven and hold the stuff for her.–

+Be careful. Maybe is here.+

–I didn't say nothin' to Maybe!–

The other woman said, "Maybe what? I never said they were for the oven! They were table dishes. It ain't my fault she ain't got no sense."

–You, I like, Spider Legs! Did you bring any of the crap that broke for us to look at?–

We'll have to see the product to know if it was misused.

+That's what I just said, Butt Face.+

"She might of brought some," the second woman declared. "Ain't no way I could if she tried to burn it all up!"

—I still like you, Toad Toes. What you got planned for tonight?—

+Hey! Hey! It is not proper for a judge to try to date a defendant!+

"He ain't asked you!" the woman said. "You ain't got no parts that could do me no good."

+Got you!+

—You're a woman after my own heart.—

"You ain't got no heart, neither!" she shot back.

The first woman dumped some broken and cracked pieces of crockery on the table by the throne and the golems inspected them.

+This looks like oven wear. It is ... made with too much clay and.... I find that this was probably sold as general pottery. Did she tell you it wasn't for cooking?+

"She said it was for anything. Anything includes cooking, don't it?" the plaintiff answered.

—Would you use it for shoes? What do you mean, it's for anything?—

+We were discussing the pottery and cookware. There are limits to words. It was plain she meant the pottery was for general purposes and could be used in water, for cooking and for serving. Stop being obtuse. Be nice.+

The second woman jumped in. "I didn't specifically say for cooking! We were talkin' about lots of things."

+Your sly evasion tells us what we want to know, that you have deliberately misrepresented the quality of the product. It is as much or more a lie to leave something out as it is to put something in. The court finds for the plaintiff. Order full restitution of wares or compensatory barter.+

"I ain't got no idea what you just said," she replied.

—He said you got to give her some dishes that don't come

apart in an oven or give her her money back. I *do* still like you, Honey Hugs!–

"Stick it in your nose, Bronze Dome," she snarled.

+I like you to!+

–You're pretty good! You also have to pay her for any of the food that was ruined when the crap broke. Want to try for building her a new house, Fats?–

The two women walked away. Z saw them laughing and talking together in the hall.

[They come mostly to listen to the golems argue. They seem to be dispensing a weird sort of justice, though.]

Tom said, "I think it's a good idea. They go away feeling good about it."

They stayed for another claim. It was about some cattle that had gotten into another farmer's gardens and ruined them.

–You got to keep the damned livestock in a fence, Chum.–

"But it wasn't all my fault! The fence was broken and I didn't know it."

+That is not important. If the animals belong to you and go onto the property of another, for any reason, you are then legally responsible for any damage. The only exception is that, if the person has given an express permission for those animals to be on his property, he assumes certain liability himself.+

"I don't know what that means!"

–Blabberpuss here likes to hear himself talk. He said you got to pay for any odd crap your animals mess up on somebody else's land. Period.–

+Don't you say that! I said there was an exception! If the plaintiff has given verbal or physical evidence of legal entry onto the property, the claim is null!+

–Go play in a volcano, Tin Tongue! You said he had to

pay for what his stock does on this other bird's property. Final! Period!–

+I said unless he had permission for said animals to enter the area! Another exception is where somebody else opens the fence. Then the person who opens the fence becomes responsible. That has nothing whatever to do with it! If the plaintiff gives his permission to enter, he assumes liability, unless it is otherwise declared before entry is effected!+

–You got to pay is what he said, Grazer Gut. So you pay. You ain't gonna stand there and argue are you? It could get expensive.–

The two farmers left.

The next case was two people who were bringing a complaint about loud parties at the home of the neighbor between them.

–How many parties you have, Superstud?–

+That is irrelevant! The pertinent question is whether or not the noise is decibellious enough or of such late duration as to constitute intervention into the rights of the several plaintiffs to have reasonable privacy and peace on their own properties.+

–Yeeez! Even I didn't get that one, Broom Breath! What the hell is decibellious?–

+Loud, No.+

"Loud, yes!" one of the plaintiffs declared. "Un ut were all night, too!"

That stopped them!

+Uh, I was referring to my colleague when I said.... Never mind. What was the duration and frequency – No wants to know that – of these alleged parties?+

"Ef'n yuh want tuh know how long un how many, thuh last un lasted fur 'most three days un two nights!" he replied.

"I don't have that many parties," the defendant offered.

"Maybe one every twenty five or thirty days."

*Excessive frequency is not the point at issue here. The extreme decibelliousness (–Sheesh!–) and duration are the actual points in contention.+

–Once a year you could get away with, Studsy. That, or invite us.–

+I believe we can handle this easily enough. The court will find for the plaintiffs. The defendant is ordered to not again have any parties or other forms of activities that will cause abnormally high degrees of decibelliousness (–Gah!–) past the line of his own property. Should you again do so, you will be found in contempt of court and will be sentenced for such.+

"Hunh?"

–He said, you get loud enough for us to hear off your own property again and you'll get a free thirty day tour of the dungeons, Hot Pants! You'd miss a whole party!–

"Ut tain't 'is propitty," a plaintiff said. "Ut's mine."

–Say WHAT?!–

+Are you testifying that the domicile of the defendant from which the complaint was generated is held by yourself in title?+

"Hunh?"

–Studsy Wudsy here is throwing loud parties in your house – and you bring it to court?–

"Uh, yuh. 'E's muh cousin. 'E's famly," he explained.

+I have to ask you something. I'll phrase it in the manner of my colleague, as you seem more familiar with the vernacular. If it's your property, why the hells don't you throw Hot Hooves out on his skinny ass?+

"Kin uh do thet thar? 'E tol' me uh couldn't toss ut famly. 'Twarn't legal!"

–Gunhh! Listen here, Studso! You got until this time tomorrow to get *all* your crap out of that house and off of these people's property or you get the free tour of the dungeons! Get the picture, Balloon Nose?–

+I again have to agree. You will also be held fully liable for any vandalism, harassment, or other vindictive actions youmay take!+

"Er, what? I...." the defendant stuttered.

–He says, and I will admit to agreeing, just to show you I can be as magnanimous as my colleague, you break anything or you bother anybody around there, you get the long tour of the dungeons for twice the time! Got it, Freak Beak?–

Z, Tom and Thing went out. There were people waiting to take their seats.

"I'll say one sure thing, Maita," Z said. "You've got these people personally interested in the court system! It may be great fun, but you're establishing a good basis. As funny as their act is, they're following the letter of the law!

"I hate to think there'll soon be lawyers screwing the system up."

No there won't. The golems have already made it plain no lawyers will be allowed in the courts, except for criminal complaints. Lawyers will be greatly restricted in those cases where they are used and the courts will set the fees they may charge. No lawyer may become a judge, so they won't fall into that trap! If they start a political system here, we have to leave something in place that will make it difficult or impossible for lawyers to seize the political machinery. I'm sure Z can tell you what happens when they have the whole system tied up!

[Maita?]

Yes, Thing?

[Didn't we see another castle, a large one, when we came here? Do you think Martin goes there, too?]

"I'll be damned!" Z said. "I'd completely forgotten there

was another castle!

"What was the castle like, Maita? – I mean, compared to this one."

"I see what you mean," Tom said. "If these are only a count and countess, is the other the king?"

[That's sort of what I wondered.]

The other castle is larger than this and is at a natural seaport at the mouth of the longest river on this island. There's a large town, perhaps a city, surrounding it.

"Why didn't you bring this up before?" Tom asked.

You were told of the other castle and chose this one because the mountains were so convenient. I agreed you would direct our ventures here, so was waiting for you to decide to try the other. I had no way to know you'd forgotten it.

"It's strictly our own fault, Tom," Z said. "Let's go to the other one and see what's different there. If the king's there, Martin will be there, more than here."

The group went back to their castle to make a sign, which they put on the table in the dining room saying they had gone to the castle at the seaport and would return. They told Net and Ward they would be away, then headed for the big city.

This was a strange experience.

The strange demon-wizard and the black demon had taken the magic clam shell to the capital to meet with King Lear and had left the two-headed golem to judge the court they had earlier established here at Teeme. The Countess Toot was locked in the tower room to be beheaded. Her captain of the guard was in prison.

These crazy golems, while they were – it was? – very fair and quite reasonable in their judgments, were more a sideshow than real judges. They constantly argued with one another – it constantly argued with itself? – and, while their word was quite literally law, they were funny and fun.

The golems were a couple of bronze heads on a sort of flat bronze plate that floated around. It was wizard magic.

The heads were angled slightly away from each other on the plate. While they could move to a slight extent, they were, basically, unable to see one another.

Net sat in the back of the courtroom to watch. It would be awhile before he was needed at the restaurant and his wife could handle most of that on a slow day.

Net had met the wizard – had, in fact, become friends with him and his demons. He liked them all – even the demon whose head could move to other bodies.

Net thought the wizard would leave the demon with the mobile head to keep a careful eye on the golem(s), but, apparently, the three worked as a unit and didn't separate. The wizard made the golem(s) to be the judge and to make a fool of the local wizard, Tee. They had really done that!

Boss, the wizard, and Extrx, the black demon, had even wrestled in the fountain with Ward and some of the soldiers when they defeated the wizard, Tee. Maybe, the demon with the mobile head, and Yes and No, the two-headed golem, had stayed above the playing group of assorted wizards, demons and soldiers and made remarks. The people really loved these crazy sorcerers and their demons!

Now the golem(s) were judges who were establishing a court of law where the Countess Toot and her count had been running things for years. Where the count and countess had been cruel, the golems were fair. The golem(s) were also funny in their remarks. This kind of law was new here.

The golems floated in to hover over the court bench, so everyone in the room started for a seat. Court would soon be in session and the golem head with the bigger nose, No, said, "All right you airheaded ninnies! Sit down and shut up! Court's in session!"

Yes, the bigger-eared head, said, "Please be seated.

"No, I can't understand why you insist upon being so rude. That is no way to start the day."

"Stick it in your nose, Metal Pate!" No snapped. "I ain't here to be pleasant.

"Who's our first case?"

Rube, the court official who presented the cases, brought two women to the bench and said, "This is Ellof and this is Lettie. Ellof claims that Lettie stole all the spice nuts off her trees and sold them at the bazaar."

"Ellof, did you tell Lettie, at any time, that she could use spice nuts from your trees?" Yes asked.

"Don't be such a puke brain!" No snapped. "She didn't tell her she could sell the crap!"

"No, I didn't say anything about that point," Yes said. "I merely wish to determine whether there was ever any implied consent."

"I don't know what that means," Ellof said.

"It means Yes would like to get her skinny behind off on a minor technicality, Blubber. Did you ever say 'you can have all the spice nuts you want?'" No asked.

"Don't be so negative, No," Yes said. "I merely want to be sure there was no obvious misunderstanding."

"Why don't you put your lips in solitary for twenty five years?" No said. "We could all use the rest.

"Well, Doll?"

"I told her she could have any that were on her side of the fence from the one tree that's on the edge of my little property," Ellof said.

"Them's the only ones I got!" Lettie exclaimed. "She said I could have 'em!"

"Rube," Yes asked. "Do you know the quantity of the spice nuts that Lettie purveyed at her vending stall?"

"Hunh?" the bailiff said.

"He means how many of the damned things did she sell," No said. "Why the hell can't you ask a question in normal words, Turd Head?"

"She sold maybe about ten kilos I know about," Rube answered.

"And what quantity represents the annual production of the tree against the fence?" Yes asked.

"Sheesh!" No yelled. "Can't you ever ask a straight-out question? Do you have to break out the book of seldom-used terms for this!?

"Hollow Head here means, how many nuts does the crummy tree have in a year?"

"About three kilos each tree," Rube replied.

"Before Metal Mind says it, does Lettie have any trees of her own?" No asked.

"No, please be nice," Yes said. "I also must know where there are other trees from which other people have told

Lettie she could remove the produce."

"Anybody else say you could pick nuts from their trees, Knobby Knees?" No asked.

"Everbody says I can get what I want!" Lettie declared.

"But I'm the only one who grows spice nuts in that whole section!" Ellof cried.

"It don't count you can get regular nuts," No said. "They gotta be spice nuts, Sticks."

"Please!" Yes cried. "Show a little decorum, No! This is a courtroom, not a barroom debate!"

"Shove it out your.... You ain't got one," No replied. "You gotta pay Ellof for one hundred kilos of spice nuts, Lettie Dear."

"I only took maybe twenty kilos! Uh, what I mean there, uh, ain't ... uh." Lettie cried.

"It's what is known as compensation for extreme distress and duress," Yes said.

"Well I ain't payin' her fer no hunnert kilos!" Lettie snapped.

"Heater Head here means you got to pay for the trouble you caused *and* the nuts you stole," No replied. "You don't have to pay for any of it, I-beam."

"Well, I ain't! That's sure!" Lettie said.

"'Course, you're gonna have to stay in the pen nights and wash the streets with a hand brush days 'til you do pay her," No said sweetly. "Still sure, Lover Lips?"

"You can't make me!" Lettie cried.

"Rube, place Lettie in a secure detention area until the arrangements are made for compensation," Yes said.

"Hunh?" Rube said.

"Throw the skinny idiot broad in the dungeon 'til she comes to her senses – or 'til she starts scrubbing the public streets in the morning," No said. "Ain't that a lot easier to say than all that 'detention' and 'compensation' crap? Put a guard on her tomorrow to see she does a good job on the gutters."

"Do we give her meals?" Rube asked.

"Sure," No replied. "Roast a kilo or two of the spice nuts for her.

"Next case?"

"You can't eat spice nuts like that!" Rube said.

"You ever tried?" No asked.

"No," Rube replied.

"Call it an experiment," No said. "Next case!"

"I'll pay for the damned nuts!" Lettie cried.

"I figured you might," No said. "If she pays, let her go. If I see you in this court again, Skinny Dip, you'll scrub every gutter in this town!

"Next case!"

"No, please try to control your tongue!" Yes said. "That is no way to treat a citizen!"

"Aaah, shut the hells up, Dung Breath!" No cried. "She's a cheap thief! Why not call her one?

"Next damned case, damn it!"

Rube brought a soldier out.

"This is Private Wait," he said. "He assul, er, assal, er, beat up his captain."

"That is a military matter," Yes replied.

"He wasn't on duty, so it's a civil matter," Rube argued.

"Where is the plaintiff?" Yes asked.

"Uh, you mean the captain?" Rube asked.

"Yes."

"He's not here," Rube said. "He said it was open and shut and he couldn't take the time."

"Oh, he did?" No said. "Did you tell him the plaintiff is required to appear in court to face the accused person?"

"Yes," Rube replied. "He said it don't matter none for a captain. All a captain has to do is call a cop and tell him about it and the courts will sentence the guy that did it."

"Private Wait," Yes said. "Tell me what happened."

"Who the hell cares?" No shouted. "The asshole captain isn't here, so there ain't a case. Just dismiss it!"

Yes ignored No, and said, "Tell us what happened, Private Wait."

"Uh, Captain Nork came into the snack bar where my sister and I were talking and he pinched my sister on her ass so I knocked him on his."

"That about all there was to it?" No asked.

"Yes, uh, sir," he answered.

"Is your sister in the courtroom?" Yes asked.

"Uh, yes, uh, sir," he replied.

"Rube, this court orders and demands that Captain Nork appear in this courtroom, immediately," Yes ordered. "See that he is here as quickly as possible. Court is recessed until said Captain Nork is brought before the bench."

"Hey! Who the hell told you to adjourn this court, Metal Mouth!" No yelled.

"I didn't adjourn, I recessed," Yes snapped. "Just shut up!"

"Who you tellin' to shut up, Brass Ass!?"

"Please don't be so abusive," Yes said. "I apologize for snapping at you. I should not let you get on my nerves that way."

"Sheesh!" No cried.

Ten minutes later the captain was led into the court and Yes called it back into session.

"Captain," No said sweetly (Which should have been a dead giveaway, given No's usual demeanor), "Tell us what this is all about. What happened?"

The captain had a black eye and a large bandage across his cheek. "I went into this store where there was this private and a girl and I said hello to the broad and the private slugged me," Nork said.

Wait jumped up, but Rube waved him back down.

"Is the girl in the courtroom?" Yes asked.

"Yeah," Nork said. "She's right over there." He pointed to the private's sister.

"How did you say hello to her?" Yes asked.

"The regular way," Nork answered, smirking.

"Look, Chump!" No snarled. "We can bring her and ten other witnesses here to say you pinched her."

"That's my regular way!" Nork smirked even broader.

Yes said, "We find the defendant, Captain Nork, guilty of assault and battery on a female citizen. Said Captain Nork is to be taken to the dungeons and there will stay nights while doing hard manual labor for the daylight hours every day for one hundred days. The military is to be informed of this action and this court recommends Captain Nork be reduced in rank to private and that he be removed from service without honor."

"What?" Nork shouted.

"You are to be put in the pen nights and to do hard labor days for a hundred days," No said. "In addition, we tell the services to bust you and toss you out on your fat obnoxious butt!"

"You metal monsters can't make me serve no hundred days and nights! I'm in the armed forces!" Nork yelled.

"Right," No said. "We now add twenty more days and nights for contempt of court. Care to try for life?

"Next case!"

"I hate to have to admit it, No, but I agree with you on this matter, wholeheartedly," Yes said. "Physical assault by any officer of the military must not be permitted in an orderly society,"

"GHEESH! You ain't got no heart, whole or otherwise, Bong Head," No spat.

Rube brought an old woman to the bench.

"This is Fezar," Rube said. "She just wants to pet ... uh, ask the court a question."

"What is it, Mother?" Yes asked.

"I ain't your mother, and don't you never forget it!" she snapped. "I got kids of my own what's bad enough!"

"You, I like, Dreamy Drip," No said. "What's your gripe here?"

"My oldest son wants to sell my land and says I got to sign the papers 'cause he's the oldest and his pa is dead so he's in charge," she answered. "If he sells my place, I ain't got nowhere to go!"

"Did the deceased person leave a testament of property disbursement?" Yes asked.

"You don't make no sense," the old woman replied.

"Yahggh! Why don't you shut up?!" No yelled. "He means did your old man leave a will when he croaked?"

"No!" Yes cried.

The old woman shook her head at Yes and addressed No. "He said everthin' would be mine 'til I croaked, too, then it was to go to whoever I said," she replied.

"Did he write it down?" Yes asked.

"Yea!" No cried. "You finally asked a straight question! Declare a holiday! Are you feelin' sick or something?"

"He couldn't write," the old woman said.

"Then it is all yours," Yes said. "Your son has no legal claim if the respondent is spouse and the owner of record dies intestate."

"I knew it was too good to be true!" No said. "What Dung Dome means is you can tell your greedy brat to take a hike. If he tries to pressure you again, bring him to court and we'll make it plain enough he can leave you alone or spend a few years in the dungeons. If I was you, I'd make a will and leave everything to the parks department when

I croak. Leave the asshole brat one lousy centime."

"I would, but I can't write," the old woman said.

"Rube, write exactly what she asks you to for a will and we'll witness it, ourselves," Yes said. "Court is recessed for fifteen minutes."

"This is twice in one day we agree on something!" No said. "Maybe we're both sick!"

At the end of fifteen minutes Rube and the old woman came back to the bench. Rube placed the paper before the golem(s) and they read it aloud:

"I, Fezar of Tlorgport, make this will.

"When I die I want my daughter, Zambry of Tlorgport, to have all my land and all my other things except for one centime in cash for my son, Dlume of Teeme, and one copen in cash for my other son, Egar of Teeme.

"I don't leave nothing else to nobody."

Yes said, "That is hardly a proper legal document. The language is terrible!"

"What part don't you understand?" No asked.

"Oh, I understand it all," Yes replied. "It is not in proper form."

"Look, Stupid!" No exploded. "We want language that just about anyone can understand. Language that's clear. You understand it all. Which part is unclear?"

"Why, it is perfectly clear!" Yes sniffed. "That is not the point. The use of the language is atrocious."

"You make me sick, Copper Brain," No snapped. "Is that what you say exactly, old lady?"

"Uh-huh. Them's my words 'xactly like I said 'em to 'im!" she replied.

"Then this court declares this to be your legal will and we will enforce it to the letter," No said. "Rube will make a record of it. We will keep it on file and you can come back to change it anytime you want. Anyone else who wants to make a legal will can have it placed in the court's records. Rube can hire some people to run the office. After this one, a one copen registration fee to pay for the clerk or whatever."

Net saw by the sundial he should get ready to welcome the midday crowd at the restaurant, so he quietly left the busy courtroom. As he walked toward the restaurant, he thought how this system in the courts may be highly unorthodox – and even a little bit crazy, but it very well might work.

It might be the only thing that could work. While it was entertaining for the spectators, it also dispensed justice with a lot more lasting effect than the silly drawn-out litigations of the past, when the count would decree to whoever would pay him the most.

The golem(s), for all their faults, were incorruptible.

That was a plus!

It didn't take too long to reach the area. They hovered for a time, inspecting their best methods of entrance and egress.

We can land in the mountains and take a floater into town, or we can submarine, or I can orbit after dropping you off. It's all the same to me.

[Are we going in on the clam shell or on the carpet? I would suggest the sea for the clam and mountains for the carpet.]

"Sounds right to me," Tom said.

"Whatever's easiest on you, Maita," Z said.

They decided to leave the ship at sea and go into the town in the clam. Tom suggested going on the carpet from where they were, but the only pass through the mountains was long and winding and would take too long. The floater wasn't designed to go high enough to go over them. Pressurization wasn't reasonable in the thin fiberglass shell, and a force shield would be spotted by too many people. There were limits to what they would believe.

Maita went submarine and came to within twenty kilometers of the port to let the clam out, then sat on bottom in more than a kilometer of water to await their return. They went a few centimeters above the waves and up the deep river to the fortifications, such as they were, on the river's edge, then into the city. It was far too large to call a town. They got out of the clam in a park area and sent it to sit atop a large spreading tree.

Unlike the town they left, they drew a great deal of attention here. People stared and avoided them until four soldiers came to them. The soldiers were wearing silver where those in the town had been wearing bronze. The soldiers were very polite and told them to please accompany them to the government office, where the rules and laws would be explained to them – laws such as the one that forbid sorcerers from bringing demons into the limits of the city. The soldiers weren't at all discourteous and seemed genuinely curious about the demons and the floater.

The group were taken to a building directly connected to the castle and ushered into a bright cheerful room, where a fat individual in gaudy uniform was seated at a table. They were invited to sit.

"I am called Iod," the fat individual said. "I am control officer general for Loosta – just another bureaucratic job, but I can't very well refuse it. The king wants me close.

"I have a report from the officers that you arrived from the sea in a wizard's chariot and disembarked in West Park. You are obviously from the far lands, thus do not know our law here. I wish to thank you for having the good sense not to cause trouble, as so many of the barbarians do.

"I am afraid the demons cannot stay in Loosta. Indeed, none of you may stay, as none of you are native races of this realm. If you wish to establish trade or otherwise do business, quarters will be provided on the visitors' island past the fortments in the river.

"Do you understand all this?"

Z replied, "I understand what you're saying."

"Good," Iod said. "It is what I am required to say to all outlanders. That is the law and I will enforce it to the last letter. It is a terrible pity you do not understand the language completely, as it means I will have to do my duty, but that is what I'm paid for, so I must not complain, what?

"Now! There is provision in the law for those who do not

speak the language to be shown around our city and not to be unduly harassed until it can be explained to them what the law is and what it means. It is unfortunate that you do not clearly understand the law as I explained it to you. That means I will have to spend the whole day escorting you to all the sights and places of interest in the city!

"Perhaps I can show you by pointing things out. Maybe we will find someone who can communicate with you, if we seek most diligently and carefully. That is my job – *if* you don't fully understand the language."

"Say, what?" Z said in perfect unaccented Tlorgian. "Tom, I don't understand what he means, do you?"

"What did he say?" Tom answered. "I can't understand a word of that babble! It looks like they'd find someone who speaks the farland languages! Bureaucrats!"

Iod continued happily, "As you do not speak Tlorgian, we must go out to try to find someone who speaks your language. I assume you do not speak any language from this land and no one is here from any other land, so it may take awhile.

"There is an excellent restaurant across the way, where we can ask the owner if he has seen anyone like you around. If not, perhaps at the art treasury or the theater. Some of those theater people sometimes know strange languages. We have some lovely parks. Maybe someone there will speak your language. It would be a good idea for you to *speak in your own tongue* so they could come to us and tell us they speak it. There is a chance we will find something in your language in the libraries.

"We must be diligent in our search! We must search for a solution everywhere! We must never stint in our efforts to resolve this perplexing problem!

"That is, *if* you don't understand Tlorgian."

"We speak Maitan, guys," Z said, in Maitan. "Our guide

will show us around the whole city. I suppose he gets sores on his ass sitting around here waiting for someone to show up, so we're a very welcome change for him."

Iod waved happily, pointed at the door, they went out and across the wide cobbled street, where he bought a delicious meal for them. Only Thing couldn't eat any of it, except some meat. There were some odd sugars in the vegetables it couldn't digest. People would stare at them openly, but there was no open hostility in the looks, only curiosity.

Iod then took them to the castle, where they were shown through a large gallery of various artworks. The statuary was truly magnificent.

They were then taken to a theater where the players were doing a matinee performance of a slapstick comedy. Thing remarked that it might have stolen lines from the golems.

"Certain things in comedy are probably universal," Tom agreed.

After the play, they went to a large library, then to East Park, where Iod explained there were four parks in the city. They could talk here, because no one could come close enough to overhear – plus the fact they couldn't be seen by anyone they didn't see first.

"Where are you from?" Iod asked.

[We have a modest bit of a castle near where Countess Toot had her castle.]

For the first time it dawned on Z he didn't know the name of the town where they had built one castle and taken over another.

"Toot? Is that old harridan still terrorizing Teeme?" Iod asked.

"Not anymore," Z answered. "When we left this morning we heard she was beheaded last evening at sunset. Seems she'd tangled with one too many of the common trash, as she called them, and they wouldn't stand for any more."

"I can't say I'm at all sorry to hear it," Iod replied. "We get a lot of complaints about her, but we can't do much, because it's simply too much trouble to get there. That mountain trail is only passable for perhaps a third of the year. To go the sea route to Tlogport and around is as bad."

[I would think Martin could stop you from getting to her.]

"Martin? Why would Martin aid her?!" Iod exclaimed. "Sir Martin has established himself as the greatest friend King Lear ever had!"

"King Lear?!" Z cried. "Now, wait a damned minute!"

"I don't understand," Iod said. "What has King Lear ever done to you? He's the greatest and most loved king since the warrior king, Clestius!"

"No, no," Z apologized. "I've heard of King Lear. He's very famous. I thought he was of the old times, like Clestius. I had no idea he was living, now! This is such good news! I meant no disparity!"

Iod was obviously proud. "Why, if King Lear hadn't given orders that all were to be well-treated as honored guests here, the soldiers would've attacked your demons when you first arrived in the park! You would've been destroyed before you left the river.

"King Lear would make demons welcome if it wouldn't cause a revolt among all the sorcerers – such as your own Tee – to do so. He says the demons aren't evil. They're slaves who do only what the sorcerers command.

"There are no slaves in Loosta! If King Lear has his way, there'll be no slaves, ever, anywhere! Martin is backing him in that. Martin has been here ever since Clestius's time, you know. Four hundred seventeen years.

"You would never know it to look at him! He looks like

he couldn't be more than forty or forty five!

"I say this, because I can see your demons aren't treated as slaves, in any manner."

Z laughed. He explained, "We're all equal. It's true I'm a wizard, but I feel as Martin does. Slavery is a great wrong.

"Tee is dead. You mentioned him."

[He tried to kill Boss. Boss turned the bolt back on him. It burned him to a small handful of ashes.]

"You're called Boss?" Iod asked.

"Yes," Z replied. "That's Maybe, who spoke then. The black demon is Extrx. We're all close friends. We were friends in other places."

"Martin has said that Tee is gaining too much power, and misuses it," Iod said. "He'll be pleased to hear he won't be required to handle it, personally.

"You must have an audience with King Lear. He'll want to know these things."

[I believe Martin already knows.]

"Oh?" Iod said, "How is that."

"Martin knows these things," Tom pointed out.

"True!" Iod answered. "It's too bad Martin isn't here. You would've liked to meet him. He's truly a great wizard and a great man!"

[He isn't here? That's too bad. Maybe another time.]

Iod laughed. "Not too many sorcerers want to meet Martin. Very few leave with any power," he said. "Are you sure you didn't know he wasn't here?"

Z laughed at that. "We don't really care, one way or the other. We have no fight with Martin and, if you'll ask him when next you see him, you'll find he has no argument with us.

"I'm a wizard, not a sorcerer. Extrx has power of his own. He's neither sorcerer nor wizard.

"You'll find, if you check, we returned those demons

held by Tee to their own worlds. We've all been slaves, ourselves, except for Extrx. We're, therefore, very strongly opposed to slavery. You'll find that we, like Martin, would teach the young about the powers of the world around them."

"That's good," Iod said. "If you'll come with me, I may be able to arrange for you to speak with King Lear. He'll be most anxious to hear of the demise of that old harridan and, most particularly, about Tee."

They went to the palace's side entrance, where they were barred from entry by two guards with swords and lances. Iod had the group wait while he went inside. He returned after a few minutes with another gaudily uniformed man, who talked to the guard. They were invited in.

They went down a long hall to where Iod pushed aside some tapestries a good distance from the entrance, revealing a bronze door. He took a key from the ring he carried and opened the door to wave the group inside. He followed them in and carefully relocked the door. They followed another long but narrow hallway to a steep narrow staircase, where they ascended four flights and entered a comfortably appointed room.

There were four others in the room, three males and one female. Iod bowed slightly to the woman and to a very large powerful-looking man sitting beside her on a divan.

"Your highnesses, gentlemen," Iod said. "These are some peoples from far lands. They do not speak Tlorgian, but wish to bring some news and messages to King Lear. Those messages are personal and private. I will take full responsibility for their words and for all actions. I assure there is no danger to King Lear nor to anyone else.

"I must remain as translator and arbiter. If your majesty will permit?"

"Certainly," the large man answered. "I will speak again

of these matters. Another time. Leave us."

The two other men looked around the little group with open hostility. "They are demons!" one of them cried. "Surely My Lord does not wish to be here alone and undefended against demons!"

"You are a fool, Synad," Iod said. "Do you really think I would take responsibility, if there was any danger, whatever, to our king?"

The large one laughed. "You're so right, Iod." He turned to the two others. "I would that you leave, as requested. I can remove you, myself, if you refuse."

The two stamped from the room. Iod followed and watched until they were down the stairs.

"King Lear, Wald, this is Boss, Extrx and Maybe. They're recently from Teeme. They have news that, I'm sure, will delight you," Iod said. "My friends, this is King Lear and his friend, Wald."

King Lear laughed, and announced, "As you're from the far lands, you aren't my subjects. Call me Obe. My very good friend, Iod, is one of the few people I can completely trust, here.

"What's the news, Boss?"

"You may speak Tlorgian, fellows," Iod said. "Obe knows I wouldn't know about any news if you didn't speak the local language. He's not nearly so stupid as those two who were here."

"Pleased to meet you," Z said. "I've heard much about you, most of it good. That's a pretty rare thing, in itself.

"The main point Iod wants us to tell you is the sorcerer Tee is dead. The second is the Countess Toot's also dead. We took care of Tee, but the people of Teeme handled Toot in their own way."

"Tell me about it," Obe requested.

"Toot was beheaded after a trial conducted by the Teeme

townspeople. That was last evening," Z said. "We weren't there, but have no doubt the court carried out its sentence. Tee was killed when some of his sorcery backfired on him."

"What do you mean, 'backfired?'" Obe asked.

[He tried to strike Boss down with some kind of energy bolt and Boss turned it back on him. He was a pile of ashes last time I saw him. The fire he sent was returned to him.]

"You personally observed this?" Obe asked.

"We all did," Tom said.

"I'm pleased to hear all of this, if it's true," Obe said. "You must realize, we find it hard to trust demons, as they're far too often used by sorcerers in trickery."

Z grinned and said, "No one uses Extrx or Maybe. They're free demons. We're friends and partners."

He thought of all that the crystal told him about sorcery, and found his solution. "I swear on the wrath of Martin these words are true, both of my own and of my friends here."

"That's a strong oath," Iod said.

"Yes. We have nothing to hide in any of these things," Z replied.

"Is the count also dead?" Wald asked. "I have heard he's capable of the worst tortures, though Toot is known to be far the worse at inflicting pain and misery on her people."

"He died before Toot's eyes," Tom said. "She didn't seem to notice. She was only angered because she was in a room full of commoner trash."

"That sounds like the old ... yes, well," Obe said. "It's too bad Martin isn't here at this time.

"Would you have sworn the oath had he been?"

"Of course," Z responded. "It wouldn't have been necessary. I'm quite sure Martin knows these things before we can bring the news all this distance. As soon as they happen, as a matter of simple fact."

Obe laughed and agreed. "My guards told us of your amazing flying chariot," he said. "They also told us that you were very cooperative with them, which isn't a usual thing with most of the sorcerers. Did you know Martin gave them safeguards?"

[No. The safeguards wouldn't work against us, though that isn't a problem. We are a law-abiding group.]

"You would challenge Martin's magic amulets?!" Iod exclaimed.

"Yes," Tom said. "We've never had any disagreement with Martin. His defenses aren't needed with us."

Obe had been watching carefully since Thing said they couldn't be stopped by Martin's defenses. He looked warily at Iod, who was very nervous.

"What are you doing!?" Iod cried.

[Nothing. It's a fact. I don't think Martin would mind our saying what is merely the truth.]

"Are you wishing to challenge Martin?" Wald asked, interested.

"No!" Tom cried. "Please! Maybe was only stating a fact. We have no argument with Martin and we don't seek one. We feel Martin's done many very great things for Tlorg. We feel that he will continue to do so. You'll find that we look up to Martin and we've tried to do those things of which he would approve. The fact we have some powers of our own doesn't imply in any way we have any desire to start some silly power struggle with anyone. We'd rather work with the one who's done so much."

"Would you agree to a test of your powers?" Obe said.

[If it's only a test of our powers, yes. If it's a silly contest of some kind with Martin, no. We quite truly wish for no such contests.]

"It's only a test," Obe replied, "though it was made by Martin.

"Martin left a little box, which he said anyone who truly has exceptional powers will be able to, first, say what's inside and, secondly, open it.

"It'll take study. Even Martin admits that. Will you attempt to do this test?"

Z took the box and examined it, then put it on the floater and closed his eyes.

"Speak in Maitan and make it look like incantations," he chanted and made several passes over the box. "Maita can see what's inside and speak through Thing."

[X-rays show a power symbol made of gold and shaped like a six-pointed star,] Thing chanted.

"How does the box open?" Tom chanted.

[It has a catch pin attached by a wire to the lower left corner which is held by an energy field I can break easily as soon as you lift it from the floater.]

"Well done," Z finished and looked at Obe. "The magic box contains a golden symbol of Clestius the Second."

He picked the box up and placed a fingernail against the corner. He flicked the nail and the top sprung open as he said, "Abracadabra!"

He handed the open box to Wald, who took the trinket out and looked, awestruck, at the group.

"Only Martin could open the box!" she cried. "He said this himself!"

"That was true when he said it," Tom said, "It was a test. He knew that someday someone would be able to open the box. I will say – and you may think it trickery, though I *do* assure you it's not – that no evil power on the world of Tlorg could have opened that box!"

"It would be like Martin to have a spell that would show the worker of his spells wouldn't be evil. That's true," Iod agreed.

"Yes," Obe agreed. "I have no least fear of these demons if they've passed a test of Martin's. Had they meant evil, I'm sure they would've been destroyed when it opened."

"That's true!" Wald cried. "It would be so like Martin to leave a test that was a trap to evildoers! They would have been destroyed *before* they opened it!"

They talked for awhile until Obe had to leave to open the court. They said their goodbyes, then Iod walked back to the park with them, after they closed and resealed the box. Maita was able to reactivate the energy field, as there was a small circuit in the box itself for that purpose. Z called the floater down and Z toasted to friendship with Iod with some of the superb wine Maita supplied on the table. They then went back to Maita and to Teeme.

They took the carpet floater from the castle and went to check on their golems. As they entered the courtyard, they saw there were far too many people waiting to enter the building. Rube saw them and took them inside, where the crowd in the courtroom were enjoying a good laugh.

"What's going on?" Tom asked.

[The golems have a new kind of civil court going.]

"I'd say it's gotten out of hand," Z said.

[Maita agrees. It's going to do something about it.]

They went closer to where they could hear and see the proceeding. Ward was looking harried to the point of explosion while two women were in front of the golems.

"...and that cheap whore's trying to steal my husband!" one cried.

–So? When did this court get into marriage counseling? Listen, Airhead, take this crap somewhere else. We ain't got time for this stuff.–

+This is not court business. Leave.+

"It'll be court business if I kill that slut!" the woman shouted.

–Yeah, I agree. You kill her and it'll be the court's business to sentence you to beheading. You might take a good look at your husband and see if he's worth the trouble before you do that, Blubber Butt!–

+Take it to someone else. Next case.+

"I won't leave until you tell that trollop to leave my husband alone!" she screeched.

–Okay. Leave her husband alone. You happy now, Sweetums? There will be a five copen charge to you for bringing a frivolous charge, Honeycakes.–

"I ain't paying you no five copen fine for bringing that baggage to court!" she snapped.

+You're right. You're paying a ten copen fine. Care to try for twenty? Thirty?+

"And if I don't pay?" she asked, sneering.

–Then you'll spend ten days in the dungeons, cleaning the sanitary stuff, Loverlips!–

+I have to agree with No, as much as I hate to admit it. The time and work of this court is being wasted by all of this. From now on, anyone bringing a frivolous charge before this court will be fined a minimum of ten copens or ten days in the dungeons. Next case?+

Two people in a row dropped charges, then the third, an old woman, went to the bench.

–What's your gripe, Mama?–

"I want to know if I have to pay for the army protection anymore. It's just a question! I'm not making a charge here against nobody!"

+Pay? For army protection? Against what?+

–Yeah, who says you got to pay?–

"The guard soldier, Teenah, says everybody has to pay a copen a week if they live out our way. I know that isn't so much, but none of us have much out there."

+Ward, bring this Teenah character here. Now.+

−You got anybody else with you that lives out the hells wherever you're talking about?−

"Yes. There are three of us who came together and one who was here that I saw."

−All you birds from way the hell out there come right up here.−

+Will any neighbors of this woman or anyone else who has a complaint against one Guardsman Teenah come forward?+

−That's what I said, Butter Brain.−

They waited for a few minutes until Ward marched a tall guardsman to the bench.

−You the one they call Teenah?−

"Yeah. So what?" the soldier said.

+So five days in the dungeons for contempt of court, to start.+

−Mama? This the Teenah you talked about?−

"Yes sirs."

+Are all of those now before the bench complainants against this man?+

Ward answered, "Yes."

−Okay, hotshot! You got five charges of extortion filed against you. What do you have to say for yourself?−

"You can't do nothin to me! The guard got a right to make something on the side!" he cried.

+Not through illegal methods. Did you take extortion money from these elderly people?+

"If you mean did I charge them for my services, yeah," the soldier said.

−What services, Lead Butt?−

"Guarding them."

+From what?+

"From what guards guard people."

–Call the jury in the morning. He stays in the dungeon until the trial.–

+The defendant is remanded in custody until court is in session in the morning.+

–That's what I said, Dung Breath!–

+The plaintiffs will stay at Net's boarding house at the court's expense until dispensation is made.+

–Crap! Can't you talk normal, Null Noggin? This court's adjourned until tomorrow.–

The group talked awhile with Ward and Rube, then went to the castle. They went to Maita to clean up. They found a note in the hall across from the cargo door: "I see you opened the test box. I thank you for reclosing it. M."

No one said anything for a few minutes, then Z started to giggle. Tom joined in. Even Thing was enjoying it. It was good to know Martin had a sense of humor!

Tern looked over his students and felt a glow of pride. Especially for the girl, Verona! She was an absolute genius. That was definite. That was unquestionable.

So. Times change, people change, ideas change and all in the world changes. That is what life is all about.

To find a new sorcerer, one of those charlatans he had so fought against, to be one who could stimulate young minds to a voracious appetite for learning was the greatest change for him. The fact he wasn't so sure whether or not he believed in magic was an equal change.

What was Verona doing now? Putting her lenses into a tube and looking at the sky?

She was writing everything she did and observed into her notebook. She was very good at drawing, and was meticulous in her notes. The drawings were so well-done he had no trouble whatever identifying her discoveries when he repeated her experiments.

That demon, Maybe, was so very strange, yet his arguments were intelligent and considered.

Another great change. Tern arguing with a demon, even forming something akin to friendship! Maybe had a strong mind and they shared a desire to see the young learn.

Extrx scared Tern without Tern knowing the reason. Perhaps the feeling that very close to the surface in the demon was a terrible violence. There was that in the demon's nature that seemed to Tern to be a very carefully controlled fury against something. Of course, it as well could be exactly what it appeared. Taking violence and cruelties against any of the Tlorgian people as a personal affront.

There was absolutely no reason to mistrust these demons.

Indeed, his trust of Boss was fairly complete. To then mistrust Extrx was foolish! It was known he had met King Lear in Loosta and rumor had it they had passed a test constructed by Martin, himself!

That was a confusion which must be resolved. Martin said there was no magic and Boss had shown that magic was perhaps the most important factor in instilling a desire in the young to know. This was a confusion with which he was not prepared to grapple. There was too much yet to sort through.

This system, under which the question was important while the answer was secondary, was another very new thing to be considered. He was no longer a young man with the mental flexibilities youth held.

A beggar who had been sitting under a nearby tree caught Tern's eye and signaled for him to come over. He was about to turn away, as there was no reason for anyone to beg here since the demons and their wizard opened the chests of the castle and had made provision for anyone who needed to earn. The truly disabled and infirm were not required to work, but would be provided for.

Then he saw the ring. It was Martin, himself, who simply didn't want to disturb the childrens' study.

Tern went to sit on the bench beside Martin.

"I note you've been instructed in the methods that will make the young wish to learn," Martin said. "It makes me wonder if you can see what I have done?"

"I am confused," Tern replied. "You said there is no magic. Boss seems to have shown the children that, indeed, there is."

Martin laughed and smiled. "My friend," he replied, "I didn't say there was no magic! I said there were no *answers* in magic! Is that not true, my friend?"

"Yes, but you...!" Tern replied. "I see! Boss taught that

answers are of no importance. Only the questions."

"And magic has no answers for another reason, my friend," Martin said. "I've noted your confusion about the differences in what Boss and I have said.

"Tell me, now, could you not see how I was saying the very definition of magic was a thing without an answer? If one has the answer the magic is gone!

"I'm sometimes too subtle, but you should have seen that. I made a mistake by being overly subtle with you. It has held you back, I'm afraid. You have a very literal mind.

"I wish to tell you it is good that Boss has stimulated the genius in Verona. You've learned a great lesson in teaching. You must do things to find each student's special interest, then you must stimulate that interest. This, I've always said.

"There *is* magic, my friend! There is a great magic in that girl's genius!"

Tern thought for a moment, then smiled to himself. "And you, my friend, know me well enough to know I recognize a complete fraud when I see one. The fact you said there is no magic as an absolute statement, which you did, despite your protestations to the contrary now, meant I would have proven you wrong.

"I do not like absolute statements!"

Martin again laughed. They chatted for a moment, then Tern asked, "Did Boss solve an unsolvable puzzle?"

"Yes, my friend, he did," Martin answered. "It was not meant to be unsolvable. It was solvable only by one who had the true good of all of Tlorg's people in his heart."

"And the demons?" Tern asked.

"They're each as good of heart as Boss," Martin replied. "The demon, Maybe, is more compassionate than Boss or Extrx, who have personal motives. Maybe has none. It simply cares."

"Extrx is, then, not to be trusted?" Tern asked.

"You do not like rodentstalkers or other cats," Martin replied. "Extrx reminds you of them. You feel they are all inherently cruel and sneaky, so now wrongly put those feelings against Extrx.

"Extrx has no ulterior motives. His rage, held in check, and his propensity for violence, which you intuit, are against the ideas of slavery and against such as the late count and countess, who they have seen fit to rid us of – or to have us rid ourselves of, in any case.

"The motives of Extrx and Boss relate to me. They are a good force, or they couldn't have solved the puzzle box."

"I believe you will not explain their motives to me," Tern replied. "They are from far worlds, as Boss said? Other worlds that are this one in another place?"

"Yes. Other worlds," Martin said. "The Fromes are the most common called here from other worlds that are this one. They are a very good people. There are the Targ and Plutons, all of different worlds that are this one. There are the Meesorchii, who are much like the Fromes, but are rarely found here. Tee called several, by accident. There are many such worlds that are this one. There are many that are not this one.

"I came to tell you I must go to one of those other worlds, myself, soon. I won't longer be here very much. You are a special friend and you're a teacher. Much of the future is in your hands. You must realize the potential of one such as Verona and must keep her interested until her desire to know is a habit she cannot break!

"There is some chance we will not again meet. I wished to wish you well."

"And I wish you well," Tern said. "I will swear on the wrath of Martin I will always do my utmost to see that Verona and all others develop a strong desire to know. It is my calling and my purpose. It is what I do."

Martin put a hand on Tern's shoulder and squeezed, then walked from the square. Tern returned to his students. Verona had two prisms and was mixing the bands of color. She was carefully writing her results in the notebook.

Z picked the note off the wall and asked, "Did you detect the fact Martin was aboard this ship, Maita?"

No. Are you sure he was?

Z looked exasperated. "The note's hanging in the hall you can't get to unless you open the cargo doors and come into the hold or, at least, the emergency port – which you've sealed! After that, you've got to open the door to room one to get into the hall.

"Yeah, I'm pretty sure he was here. The note might maybe be called a clue to my decision."

It would be one hell of a sight easier if you simply TPed the note into the ship and against the wall.

"Why not leave it in the castle, then?" Z asked.

[Because only we could find it, here.]

"Nobody said he couldn't have put it there in person," Tom said.

"Maybe not, but I think he's looked over this whole ship," Z said.

[And if he has?]

"Nothing," Z answered. "I don't mean to say he'd go to all the trouble to leave the note in here just to mystify us and show he could. That would be something he isn't. Petty.

"I think he was here and left the note to honestly thank us for not screwing up his test."

You may be right, but I don't think even Martin could get inside this ship without me knowing.

"What's really the difference?" Tom asked. "I don't want to meet Martin face to face. I think he knows that. Not under these circumstances. Maybe, someday in the future, when I need some magic, but not now.

"I'm much like Tranz. I think I want to get out of here pretty soon. I know what Tranz was afraid of. I know why he didn't want to take the chance of meeting Martin. If we do meet him, we mustn't tell Tranz anything. I mean that."

[Now you confuse me, again. I didn't think I understood why you were doing this at first, then I thought I did, now I think I don't.]

"It all has to do with something Z said on the ramparts when we first came here," Tom explained. "Do you remember, Z? About robbing the future? About the kids?

"What will happen to me if I meet Martin? I think he knows that. I think I will *not* meet him. Not here, and not now.

"I think we should finish what we've started about the courts. I think Z should talk some more with the teacher. Then I think we should get the hell out of here!"

I admit I don't know what's going on. I know you two think this is of ultimate importance to these people and that you have been reverting to childhood fantasies. I thought the whole object was to meet the being who shaped your individual races so meaningfully.

"It was. Accent on *was*! We've been living in our own little fantasy world," Tom said. "It s been great fun, but now the fear comes."

"I'm not so sure I know what you're talking about, Tom," Z said.

"We've both reverted to those childhood fantasies, now, Z," Tom explained. "If you come face to face with the reality? What if Martin/ Frezzwin is simply a brilliant scientist? What happens next time you need to escape?

"I said I'd accept death before I'd accept the stealing of those legends from Zeena's children. If I meet Frezzwin, will they be taken from *me*? Where will my legends go? Can any being possibly be what I want, indeed, desperately need, that legend to be?

"No! I want to get out of here!"

"I see what you mean," Z agreed. "I never thought of it. I was having too much fun."

[What does this really mean? You said you know Martin won't come to face you.]

"Yes, but what happens when we finally do something that makes it imperative that we meet?" Tom said. "We'll have to sacrifice ourselves, as will Martin, in the event *not* doing so will harm these people."

That's too true. Shall we start withdrawing from influence in the morning?

[How are you going to leave? What will happen to the new courts without the golems?]

I can handle that part. Get some rest and we will do some things tomorrow. I'm not saying that we will leave here tomorrow. That would be unconscionable.

"I agree," Tom said. "We must disentangle ourselves as quickly as we can, though."

They agreed to discuss it in the morning and each went to his own private spot on the ship.

Z laid back in the pilot's chair and adjusted it to where he was most comfortable.

"Maita?"

Yes, Z?

"I'm in another stew."

What do you mean?

"I feel pretty foolish about all this. I mean, what was it really about? What did we accomplish?

"Sure, we had a lot of fun. We got to act like kids. It was good therapy, but how much have we lied to ourselves? I mean, did we do any good here?"

We did no harm and we might have done some good.

"I suppose we did some good here, but the effects will

die out in a few years. We got rid of a sorry pair of cruel tyrants and a power-hungry sorcerer. Did we do anything that'll last, though?"

I want to talk to you about that point, Z. You have done something that will possibly make you one of the legends of this world. This world will have two Merlins, if you allow it to stand. Your tales of Atlantis can happen right here. I don't think you know what you have done.

"But Maita! I haven't done anything! Sure, they have the courts. That could be a big thing, but you established the idea, not me. It would've grown in a few hundred years on its own – it will grow.

"I don't think *our* particular court system will survive, given the strong propensity of these cultures in these stages to go into corruption so fast. I hope I'm wrong, but...."

Z, I'm not talking about the courts, though I think the idea of having the so-called common people on juries will spread. Eventually Obe will hear of it. You can bet he will seize on it.

"We haven't done anything else that'd have any effect, Maita. Getting rid of Toot and Tee certainly will make a local impact, but that won't last, either."

I will ask you a question, Z. I want you to consider the implications of what I'm going to say for awhile before you say anything. You will immediately see what you have done. I want you to consider whether you wish to take credit and be another hero for this planet. Be aware you are an alien, as is Martin. The big difference being no one knows Martin's an alien. He 'grew up' in front of everyone's eyes. He was known here when he was a young teenager.

"I sure as hell don't want any credit for anything! What do you mean?"

What would have been very different on Earth if you had the telescope and the microscope in, say 100 B.C.?

"Oh, my God!"

They have them, now. The girl did as you suggested. She put two and more lenses in a tube and moved them back and forth. She can't believe what she sees. The two moons are small and far away, and she didn't even know about the smaller one, as it's too small and far away to see with the naked eye. As luck would have it, it's near the closer, larger moon now, so she found it. She saw the gas giant they all knew was a strange star by its motion. Another stroke of luck, it's tilted at the best angle possible right now to show the four rings. She used a small deep lens and another small one and looked at the cloth. She has seen bacteria in water and she found cells in plants. You can see what this can mean. She's a genius and has asked Tern about a curved mirror. These people may have huge parabolic telescopes before they can build a very large lens! I think you can see what this might mean.

"Oh, Maita! I...."

Think about it for a few minutes. I think I know what you will decide, but I don't know how you will handle it. Good night. Get some sleep.

"I just want to know how you know all of this, Maita."

We were placing sensors when we first met Tern and his students. There are three in the tree there. He always holds his classes there, unless it's raining.

"Good night, Maita."

They slept late the next morning. No one was in the dining hall when Z went in. He ate and went out to lean over the wall and watch the town below. A small floater came to sit on the wall. They were both silent for awhile.

"Maita?" Z said about half an hour later.

Yes, Z.

"What do you want me to say?"

You tell me.

"I've got to come up with something. I want to make it seem that Martin did it all."

Think of something. We are going to town to wean these people from our golems.

They went inside and the others soon came in.

"Tom, how long can you hold the inertia field thing?" Z asked.

"A couple of minutes. Why?" Tom replied.

"I can get you out of this today. When we're in the court, stay near the door to Toot's tower. Nobody goes there except the golems, so we can have a floater ready to bring you here. We'll have to play it by ear," Z said. "Just be ready to get out. The tower door hasn't been replaced since I kicked it in, so you shouldn't have any problem."

"Won't people see me leave in the floater?" Tom asked.

"The people're going to be concentrating more on what's happening inside," Z replied.

They went to the fountain, then to the courtroom and the golems, walking into the trial of the soldier who had been extorting from the old people. The old woman was the chief witness for the court, and was answering Ward's and the golem's questions.

"...made us pay a copen a week for the protection," she said.

"What would happen if you didn't pay?" Ward asked.

"You would go out and find your eggs all broke or some birds dead. Maybe your gardens would get pulled up," the old woman replied.

–Did any of this actually happen, or would you just have this scum threaten it, Moms?–

"It happened to me!" another witness cried. "That frumpf killed my pet crawler! I saw him!" The witness was another old woman who had a cane which she was waving wildly around.

+Do you have any proof?+

"I got a foot what ain't gonna ever be right agin! He broke it! My neighbor saw him!"

−Is your neighbor here, Slim?−

"My neighbor! He's dead! He died that night! Seems he went walkin' along the cliff − climbed up an fell off − and him with the no-breath and a bad ticker! Hah!"

+Are you saying that Teenah murdered him!?+

"You figure it out!"

−Teenah, come forward.−

The soldier came to the front and glared at the golems. "You ain't got no right to keep me here! I stayed in that lousy dungeon all night! That ain't right!"

−Was it right to kill that old man?−

"Ahh, he would've died before long, anyhow. He was old. He warn't no use to nobody," he replied.

+You are admitting that you killed him?+

"Yeah. What's the big deal? He was old," he sneered.

−I direct the jury to find this man guilty of deliberate murder! Go deliberate and give us your verdicts. Ward! Slap this rock toad in irons. Now! You're as good as dead, you ... you...!−

+I am in the position of having to agree with No again.+

Z started to stand and Thing said, [No! Z. Sit down and shut up!]

"But a judge can't do that!" Z cried. "He was being tried for extortion, not murder!"

[He admitted to wanton murder. In doing so, he has as much as also admitted to crippling that old woman and extorting from these others. He shows no remorse and, indeed, doesn't seem to know he has done anything out of the ordinary. What is it you think we should be trying to teach these people? I thought you made some snide remarks lately about those phony liberal snobs of the sixties. This isn't Earth, where you can do anything, admit it, then get some halfassed idiot to defend it for some illogical and unintelligible reason. We have a pathological sociopath here. This is a new court and a new place for the court and a new law. You should sit down and shut the hell up!]

"Thank you, Thing," Z said. "I deserved that."

"I can't believe you were actually planning to defend that thing up there," Tom said. "It's an unmoral entity and should be removed from the company of people."

The jury came in and sat.

–Ward, just give me the average crap.–

Ward talked to the jury and said, "All the holdings of the defendant are to be seized and distributed to the older people in the out section. The defendant has been recommended for an average sentence of twenty five years of imprisonment. All the members of the jury agree this is a true reading of their recommendations."

+So stated. The judges concur in all particulars.+

"What's that supposed to mean?" Teenah asked.

–It means that Ward is to take you out that door into the courtyard and run a sword through your heart as many times as is necessary to ensure you are dead, dead, dead. Now!–

"Now?" Ward asked.

+See that all who do not wish to see this thing are first cleared from the courtyard, as well as all minors – whether they want to see it or not. Tell the rest of the guards we are now going to investigate their actions and, if they have done any of the same kind of things, they had better start running. Now!+

–Now I got to agree with Yes. You can guess how deeply

that hurts.–

They waited until the court had finished for the day and called Ward and Rube aside so Thing could talk with them in the back rooms about how to continue the court. There were still a full room of people when Z called, "Can I have your attention?"

They looked at him and he continued, after signaling for Tom to go to the door behind the bench. "I'm afraid some of the things we've started here are now going to be under your own supervision. These courts are a gift from Martin. Without his being here, there would be no courts and you'd still be under Toot the Ugly and the evil sorcerer, Tee.

"These things are to be your responsibility. I'm here because Martin is here. I'll soon be gone.

"Extrx will go now. His job is done.

"Extrx, go back to your place, my friend! Go with our love and our blessings!

"Alacarazam!"

Tom disappeared. The people gasped.

The golem floater came to hover over Z's head.

+Our job, also, is done. Only Boss and Maybe have yet to do some things in honor of Martin.+

–Long live the name of Martin. We have enjoyed our time among you and hope we were used to teach you something important.–

+Remember our lessons. Goodbye friends.+

–Goodbye, friends.–

The floater went out the front hall and shot into the sky.

"Maybe will stay here to help set up the court system. I'm sure Martin will be proud of the way you carry it on. We're as sure you will build a good system that's fair to all citizens," Z continued. "I've enjoyed being among you. I consider you my friends."

Z went out and to Net's, where he ordered the stew and the wine with sweetcakes. Net came to sit with him and Tern came in a few minutes later.

"I'm going away, guys. I'll never see any of you again," Z said. "I'll really miss all of you. I'll miss Fane's stew and her sweetcakes. We've had some fun and, I think, have learned a bit from one another in the process."

"You're not really going?" Net protested.

"Yes, I'm afraid so," Z replied. "My job here is done – almost. I have to go."

"But you are so good for the students!" Tern cried. "Your lecture on the lenses! Do you have any idea how much little Verona has done? All because of you?"

"I meant to start a certain type of idea in the younger children," Z said. "Do you have any idea how intelligent that child really is? She's a genius!

"I meant to make these children think for themselves, I didn't know. She'll advance this whole world more than you can guess. She's found the second moon! Only Martin and I knew of it.

"You, Tern, will be remembered as her teacher for many thousands of years. You must write all about her, what she discovers, what she learns, what she can teach. She'll be almost as famous as Martin, himself, and that's precisely what he wants. He has wizardry on his side, and Verona has science on hers.

"This is as Martin has told you. Science can explain most things. You must keep her and the others prodded into wanting to learn."

"I promise you that," Tern answered. "My only claim to fame would be that I was the teacher to a famous person. I won't miss that opportunity for immortality.

"I should tell you I have recently spoken with Martin. He showed me where he didn't tell me there was no magic, but simply that magic had no answers, because, once the answer is known, the magic is gone – by definition.

"I will not miss fame. I would miss teaching, I think."

"Yes you would," Net said. "You were born to teach, so teach, you will. You wouldn't do anything else, even if you could."

They all laughed. Tern said he had to get back to the students, and asked that Z come with him to give them some more ideas before he left.

Z went into the back to say his goodbye to Fane, then went with Tern to the tree, where the students were waiting. They were glad to see Z, and ran to him. They asked where Extrx and Maybe were. Z explained that Extrx was already gone and Maybe was helping to get the court system properly set up. They were all sorry the golems were gone, because they were always funny.

"They taught some very serious things by being funny," Tern said. "Martin would think of that."

Z didn't correct him.

Verona said she had seen things moving in a small drop of water through her lenses. She had seen a star with rings around it, too. Z explained that it was another world, and suggested Tern use his numbers to find exactly which bodies were moving around which other bodies. If she studied the ringed planet for a year, she should be able to see where the focus of the circle was. He explained that gravity force acted like light from the lens.

Some of the other students asked questions and he tried to suggest answers to them in such a way they would think of many more questions. They talked all afternoon before Z returned to the castle as it was getting dark. Thing said it had a whole lot more to talk over with Ward and Rube, as it was all being written down, now they had to check to be sure it was correct. Z suggested they come back in the morning, as Ward and Rube could use the rest.

They arranged for the juror who seemed most open-minded and fair to act as judge on the following day and Thing was to watch to be sure they did it properly.

Z and Thing went to the castle, where Tom was waiting. He had taken what he wanted to keep into the ship. Maita had taken most of the castle down. It was no more than a shell. The plan was to take the shell away by releasing the anchors and using the ship as a tug. The castle could be carried into space and dropped into the sun. The interior had been run through the elementizer and reduced to its basic atoms, which had been blown into a cave nearby, after Maita refilled its bins with those elements it needed. They agreed to do that the next night, as they would have to be there tonight.

They cleaned up, ate a good meal, and met in the pilot's dome to talk over the situation.

"I don't think we did any damage here," Tom said. "Maita explained about teaching the girl about lenses and some bits about astronomy a couple of thousand years early. Maybe this race has an unusual potential, anyhow. Look at King Lear. He's way ahead of his time.

"I wanted to ask you about your reaction when you first heard his name, Z."

"King Lear was a play back on Earth by one of the greatest playwrights of all time," Z said. "What, with all our magic and stuff, I just wasn't ready for it. The play we saw when we first got here sounded almost like it could have been written by the same playwright. One of the rarer demons here is the Pluton, from Hades. Those are all Earth terms!"

[Was he a king in the magic era?]

"Not in the time of Merlin, no," Z answered. "Magic was still a big thing at the time of King Lear, though, because it was at the time the play was written."

I just want to say this is the first time we have ever considered leaving a place where we haven't managed to accomplish what we set out to do.

"Bull," Z replied. "We left Empire Center for a couple of years and went back there because we felt guilty for leaving those planets in slavery."

[What do you think will happen? Will we come back here? Will any of this last?]

Perhaps, in a couple of hundred years. I want to see the results of Z's little scientific prod.

"Do you think we've disrupted Martin's plans here?" Tom asked.

"I think Martin was about ready to leave here," Z said. "The legend's fairly well established and the race has been steered along a path that'll eventually lead to something. The hiding of the planet was a last effort to cast the legend deeply enough that it would survive.

"Martin's been here four hundred years. That's about the time he spent on Earth, I guess. I think he spends his time on a number of planets. He's got something like the transmat, so no time is lost in going from place to place. He can even spend four hundred years here at the same time he spends four hundred years on other planets. I don't doubt he was working on several worlds while he was on Earth."

"And on Zeena," Tom agreed.

[I didn't once hear the hiding mentioned. If it was to be that important, why not?]

"Because everyone knows why it was done, so there's really no reason to discuss it." Tom said. "There was some reason for night to be done away with for a few days, so Martin did it."

[But what?]

We probably won't know for a long time.

"We already know," Z corrected.

[We do?]

Z leaned to the console and picked up a crystal laying there. He put it in the socket.

"Of course," he said. "Tee knew, and we read him. It's on the crystal we.... Ah, it was because the black elementals of the mountains on the mainland would be driven from the world if night were abolished.

"Martin's one basic reason for existence was to destroy the black magician, therefore, the black elementals. It would forever free the peoples of Tlorg from being slaves to the whims of sorcerers and their evils.

"It was done. For twelve days the sun didn't set and there was light! The black powers were defeated and can now only be called up in small ways.

"It's prophesied that Martin will now retire to roam the mountains. He'll see that the black powers don't again become too strong. That's why he wasn't at Loosta. He's gone to the continent. He'll return when and if he wishes."

Why didn't the people talk about it?

[Aren't you reading the crystal? Speaking of the black powers can call them forth. The people have agreed not to mention them for a period of ten years, so they'll lose all their strength. The people won't call them, so they'll grow ever weaker.]

I suggest you all get some rest and we can finish here tomorrow. It seems we came here just in time to interfere with Martin's travel plans, so he will appreciate it if we go away. I suspect he stayed a little longer only because we showed up. This also explains several things, such as our reception in Loosta. They would expect the greatest sorcerers from the continent to come to pay respects to Martin. He freed them from the direct slavery to the black masters.

Tom stood and agreed, then went to the elevator. He turned to Thing, who said, [I will stay with Z here, if he doesn't mind. It's far better than staying alone tonight, I think.]

Tom went down (up?) to the main floor and to his bunk in room nine, while Thing curled into a ball on Z's lap. Maita turned the lights down and they slept.

In the morning Thing and Z went back to the castle to watch the new judge conduct a couple of short trials before adjourning court for three days, as there were few cases, now that the entertainment was gone.

"Making people pay a fine for frivolous suits has saved us a lot of time and trouble," Ward reported. "It was a good start with the entertainment and we learned a lot, but I agree the courts are a more serious matter than all of that."

[Your future freedom lies in the success of the courts. I am not speaking excessively. That's a simple fact. They are and will be the determining factor.]

They met with Ward and Rube and spent until midday making the rules of the court. They then moved to Net's, where they continued until late in the afternoon. Tern came in and left to return with the students, who made some pretty good new suggestions. One adolescent boy was very good at choosing the right words to say a thing so it wouldn't be ambiguous. Z suggested he make a study of laws and rules and work for the court in wording the decisions in such a way future courts could use them.

[You're making a lawyer? You?]

"No," Z replied. "A court officer. This lad will become a professor of legal terms and usages, I predict. For many more centuries, his words and explanations will be read by all the local courts to establish precedents. He must be extremely careful always to keep justice and fairness foremost in his thoughts as he makes his decisions and pronouncements."

"Is that a prophecy?" Tern asked.

"It's a prediction based on what I'm seeing and hearing," Z answered.

They talked until darkness was falling, then said their goodbyes. Z made it plain they would most probably not be back, then he and Thing got on the carpet for a last ride up to the shining castle on the cliff.

Tom was leaning on the rampart when they came in. He said, "I was just thinking how I would love to splash around in that fountain pool one more time."

"We can't," Z said. "It wouldn't be the same, anyhow. The play and fun is gone and this has become another job. I'm really afraid you and I are going to be leaving our childhoods behind when we leave this planet, Tom. I'm finally growing up." He sighed. "I don't like it. At all."

"I guess I feel the same way," Tom said. "How are we ever going to get this castle out of here, Maita? They'll see it, if they look."

It's a little cloudy tonight and I've sprayed the three walls behind a flat black. I have servos ready to spray the side toward the town black in a few minutes when the sun will show no reflections, anymore. The anchors are released and the cables attached. We are ready to go. The only evidence we were here will be twelve unexplainable holes in the rock base where the anchors were attached.

About an hour later Maita announced they were taking off. They rose quickly and Maita swung the castle shell in an arc that would drop it into the sun in about a year. It would never be in a position where Verona's lenses could find it.

They went to Fortney, where they spent a couple of

hours with Wahnee. They told her the planet was under a magic spell and she wasn't to worry about any planets that disappeared in the future, so long as a satellite would go into orbit around where it had been. If the satellite would orbit, the planet was there, even if she couldn't find it.

Maita decided to go to the complex that was running the empire for a short time before returning to Empire Center, then they got a couple of charged power spheres to replace the ones they'd depleted since the last refueling.

Everything seemed to be working well at the complex. They went into the main computer terminal, where Maita attached directly to the master brain while Thing and Z spent the few hours walking around and studying the amazing machine.

Here was one machine that covered an asteroid over seven kilometers thick by nine long! As Maita put it, you could put a hell of a lot of information into that much area.

Maita was, at all times, in direct contact with the machine, as, indeed, it was a part of Maita, in a way. That information was available for whatever use they felt was appropriate.

Maita said they had to make one more detour before going home. It took them to Frim, the vacation spot of the empire. It had casinos and every other entertainment imaginable. It was established long ago, when the empire was just beginning to expand (Book three: *Pirates*).

"What's the matter there?" Z asked.

We have a captain we once said, oh about seventeen or eighteen years ago, we would have to execute some day, because he was born to be crooked. It seems he's trying to establish a crime syndicate on Frim and run it from Sentah.

"Did that machine know that?" Tom asked. "And for how long did it know?"

The machine didn't know that, but it had enough of the information. We are going to confront our good old Captain Mock.

They landed at the space port where they were met by Zoo, who they had put in charge of the space port facilities. He was genuinely glad to see them.

His wife was head of education for the entire planet.

"What's this we hear about Mock?" Tom asked.

"You won't hear anything about Mock anymore," Zoo promised. "It seems his ship malfunctioned this morning and he was blown to the hell he deserves."

Tell me what happened, Zoo.

"Straight truth?" he asked. "Okay.

"Mock was setting up his own little deal where he could run things to his taste – you know his taste.

"I know you guys don't say nothing about the girls and that kind of thing, so long as they come here on their own.

"Well, Mock was getting girls here, and we found he had forced them into it. We tried to stop him, but he wouldn't listen. He was doing a lot of stuff like that. He put in some crooked games. That kind of thing.

"We tried to get through to him that we had a sweet setup as it was, and we were still legitimate, but he just wouldn't listen, so a bunch of us got together and decided he wasn't going to jeopardize it for all of us.

"He told us to go to hell, so he had an accident. I won't say anymore about it."

[That's fair enough. You know how we feel about having one idiot screw it up for all of us.]

They stayed the night on Frim. They left for Empire Center in the morning.

"That's like organized crime on Earth," Z said. "Their own law and their own executioners."

*They were pirates only a short time ago. It's all they

understand. It will be a long time before anyone else tries to break the system. They can't fight their own kind.*

They landed, and Tranz came out to meet them. The first thing he said after looking over Tom and Z was, "You two look older."

"Yeah," Tom said. "We had to grow up a little."

"I was afraid of that," Tranz answered. "Frankly, it was why I ran. I didn't want to grow up."

Things were running fairly smoothly for the past two months, since the group returned from Tlorg. The weather on their part of Empire Center was pleasant, being slightly cool at night and very warm during the day – which was what Z liked.

Tous had taught the youngsters well. The orchids were flourishing (And flowering, too). The bromeliads were rapidly establishing themselves, and the camellias had begun to set buds. The care they received while the group was on Tlorg was as good as Z could have done, himself. Add to that the amazing artistry of someone like Tous, who placed some of the larger camellias as a banked background for large cymbidium orchids with various odontoglossums and miltonias in the crotches of the huge spreading oak-like trees higher on the mountain, giving a riot of color in this, the winter season on Empire Center.

The temperatures were only a few degrees cooler than in the summer season. They never quite got to the point of frost until higher on the mountain.

A kilometer and a half lower, where Z had his home, was about ten degrees warmer year around. Just a bit higher, there was a small clean stream, along which Tous had planted hundreds of varieties of the lady slippers.

Tous and Bess had, after much argument, finished the new domicile in the mountains for Z. Z had to admit it was truly spectacular.

"Of course!" Tous said with his burbling giggle. "I am the finest artist in the galaxy, and Bess isn't too terribly bad, himself – for an amateur!"

"You are an egomaniacal pontificating hack and totally insufferable on top of it!" Bess snapped back.

The two great artists always acted like that. They were truly good friends.

The inlaid marbles formed a magnificent "painting," and the interior was extremely comfortable. Maita had duplicated the pilot's chair and installed it for Z as its contribution. It was identical in it's feel.

Well, naturally, Z! You lay on a 'soft' force field that extends its area of force exactly in the same manner.

Thing became entangled in its plan to make a large area of the sea bottom into a garden, so spent a great deal of time there in the daylight hours and stayed in the domicile at night, as did all the people working on the island, though all they had to do was step into the transmats to be at their homes.

[The strangler figs you planted for me on my island will be right in about twenty years. My gardens will extend clear from here to my island by then – I hope!]

Thing's personal island was about four kilometers south of New Earth, as Z called his own place.

The empire was running smoothly without their help and they were, those without special projects, spending some time on their home planets. Tom was on Zeena, romancing some girl, while Tranz was on a big boxy spaceship with his parents somewhere toward galactic center. (Though not past the limits of the empire.)

"You know how horny I am all the time," Tom had said as he stepped into the transmat.

Tranz had Maita deliver him to his parent's ship.

Maita was working on some project inside the mountain. It said it was a personal project, so the others respected that and didn't pry, though both Z and Thing were almost dying of curiosity.

Verona checked her telescope again and very carefully

drew the position of each of the small stars.

The idea of the curved mirror on the bottom and a lens to look at the mirror through a prism – if she could get the mirror more smooth, it would show so much more than anyone had ever guessed!

The moons, both of them, were just big, scarred, pitted and irregular rocks. There were moons circling the big world with the rings and there was another world with rings that was smaller or was farther away. Verona accepted the second explanation.

Borie had worked with Tern's numbers and the trigonometry thing and had said that, since the moons near Tlorg both went around Tlorg and Tlorg obviously went around Sun, the numbers would allow the ringed world to also go around Sun, which Tern said Martin agreed was true. That would, by those same numbers, mean the ringed world was big enough that more than a hundred and sixty worlds the size of Tlorg would fit inside of that world and two of the moons she had found spinning around that world were more than half the size of Tlorg! Could that be?

There would have to be a special new system of numbers to explain all of that stuff out there. Numbers, while she was very quick with them, were not her main interest, so she would leave that to Borie. Maybe he could determine if Sun was really several thousand times bigger than Tlorg.

She was fascinated with light! So much could be done with it. So many things were yet to be learned – things she hadn't even seen in her most vivid dreams! It was too bad the wizard, Boss, wasn't still here to point to the proper kinds of questions to ask.

One must make do!

Wald watched as Iod and Obe tried to communicate with

the ugly huge bird-like Frome, who was trying to learn the local language.

Dear Obe! It was so like him to outlaw the demons in the city, then, himself, allow one to stay right here in the palace where it could hide from that sorcerer, Malkite.

That was Obe, though! Should she tell him his heir was ever growing inside of her?

He knew. She could tell. He was just a little bit extra careful with her, like he thought maybe she would break or something. It was strange she held no fear of that Frome. The few times she had been there and close to it, it had been most polite, in its own way. It did try, and she could understand its sadness and pain. It was trapped here on Tlorg, and would probably never again see its home.

She didn't know what the Fromes meant when they said that everything on Tlorg was blurry and flat to them. They had tried to explain what they meant, but blurry and flat was as close as they could come.

Obe was trying to find a sorcerer with the power to send the poor thing home, but wasn't having much luck. They stuck together on those things, so there wasn't much of a chance.

If only Boss or Martin would come! It would solve the sorrowing creature's problems.

It might calm a fear she had, too. She wanted a good prophecy for her child!

The being known as Martin here on this world stepped onto the patio, nodded to Obe Lear and Iod. It addressed the Frome in its own language. He (It?) reached out to hold the big bird-like being, said, "I return momentarily," and disappeared, along with the Frome demon. About ten minutes later he (It?) stepped back. He (It?) looked to the balcony where Wald stood, and recognized she was with child. She would, quite naturally, wish reassurance.

He spoke to Obe and Iod loudly enough that Wald would hear. "Wald carries now in her womb the future greatness of the Lears," he said. That was safe enough. It would ease Wald's mind, make Obe happy, and actually said nothing. It was a statement true of any child, and Wald was healthy. The child would have every chance.

"I would like to advise you, My King, to keep a close watch and protection on the village called Teeme," he said. "There is, in that village, a girl called Verona and a teacher called Tern. There is also in that village the hope of freedom of the peoples of Tlorg for ten thousand years. This was a thing recently established by the wizard and colleague of myself known to you as Boss, who was here with his demons, Extrx and Maybe.

"Those three and their golem, of which you will hear much in the future, have established what they call a court of law. The Lears would be wise to nurture and bend to that good court over the King's Court, in many areas. The future greatness of the Lears – and even of Tlorg itself – is embedded solidly in that system, which is a thing done by those three for me.

"I return to Teeme, thence to my retirement. I am tired, my dearest friends. Take great care and the future for you is bright!"

He was then gone. It was but a step and he was in Teeme, where he watched the teacher, Tern, working with the students. He spoke with Tern for a moment, then walked from the square to the alley behind Net's Inn, where he spoke with Net and Fane.

"I must go to the Black Mountains to meditate and per- haps to remain for the rest of my life. I leave with you a prophecy, but one that is mixed.

"A child of yours, or a child of your child, will one day

become known in legend. Whether for good or evil is not clear. The choice will be of that child, determined by how he or she was raised, so take great care.

"My friends, Boss, Extrx, Maybe, and the golems have left strong legacies for all of Teeme, even for all of Tlorg.

"You are special people and I am better for having known you."

He then moved to find Ward standing near the fountain.

"Ward, there are good memories here, as well as dire warnings. Take the greatest care with the court you and my friends have created, for it holds much of the future of Tlorg within its concepts. As of now, all Tlorg is responsible for itself."

His next step placed him on a world called Neeahnah.

Bess's statue was in the center of the lake dividing Joe's People from the Tendd. He had made a large platform around it, as both races loved the water and spent some time together with friends in the lake.

Ape and Iron, two Vendans and close friends of the group (Ape having once been a member of the group) along with their two children, had just left after visiting for ten days. Z was on the hot lower end of his island, trying to coax some of the blue aganisia orchids to perk up some. The temperature at night, even here, wasn't hot enough to make them too happy, so seldom staying above the seventy five degrees all night they preferred all the time. Triss was helping him and suggesting he move them to an island right on the equator that was a few degrees warmer, though not much.

"Have you seen Joe lately?" Z asked.

He depended on Triss to "talk" to Joe, as they had a very sophisticated sign language between them and could communicate very well, even though Joe had no language.

"Yes, Z. I was with Joe and his family for a time a couple of days ago. They are doing well, and the people are still so happy to have been able to come here. They have begun to develop a culture very different from Joe's World. They are beginning to even start to build a folklore about this world and the people."

"A folklore?" Z asked. "What do you mean?"

"You know the plants with the flowers that look like little birds? They made a story they were once really birds who were hunted by the mountain hawks almost to extinction, then a great magician took pity on them and made them into flowers, where they were safe from the hawks."

"Magician?" Z said.

"Oh, yes, Z. They believe in magic and magicians," Triss replied.

"So do I, Triss," Z said seriously. "I even know a little magic."

"Yes, Z. We have magic and legends and tales of our own among the Tendd. Joe's people have a good start on forming their own. They have said the high mountains between Center Headquarters and the lake are enchanted and there is a great magic goblet on a rock in the center of the river. It was put there by a great magician and cannot be removed from the rock, except by a chosen leader. This leader will come someday from a descendant of Joe and will pick up the goblet and take it to the village. Each woman who is with child will drink from the goblet, which will never be empty for fifty years, and her children will all have the gift of speech. It is a good legend, I think. I think they must think of you as a great magician. They have named the magician after you, I think. It is strange that Joe can say the name, though, as he cannot otherwise speak very much."

Z was trembling as he asked, "What is that name, Triss?"

"The magician? He is supposed to be here and to have told them his name in person," Triss said. "It is Zeewin."